"When you ████████████████ **lingerie,** ████████████ **courage to do something you've always wanted to do, but been afraid to."**

"And you want to put this in a commercial?"

"Sure. Why not?"

"What is it the woman in the commercial wants to do but hasn't got the courage to?" he asked.

"It could be anything. Maybe she needs to give a big presentation at work. Maybe she needs the added confidence to impress her colleagues."

Jane straightened away from the desk and took a step toward him. Her heart was pounding in her chest with equal measures of fear and excitement. She let her fingers creep up the placket to toy with the top button of his shirt, even though they itched to rip the buttons from the holes and reveal the skin beneath.

"Or maybe she has the hots for her boss and is finally ready to make her move."

Dear Reader

It's funny where the inspiration for a character can come from. About halfway through the first draft of this book, my husband and I were at the local animal shelter looking for a new cat. Now, I'm a picky pet owner, so we looked for several weeks before I found the right kitty for me. During that time I met a volunteer who—like Jane—always went above and beyond the call of duty to find homes for the cats at the shelter. I knew then that I had to use her in a book. It was only later that I saw a documentary on TV about Marion Davies, a silent movies actress with a stutter who managed to make the transition to 'talkies'. I worked elements from both of those real-life people together to make my Jane, one of my all-time favourite heroines. I hope you love her as much as I do.

As always, I'd love to hear what you think of the book. You can e-mail me at Emily@EmilyMcKay.com. Or just check out the website for upcoming releases at www.EmilyMcKay.com.

Emily

HER WILDEST DREAMS

BY
EMILY MCKAY

Pamela —
Good luck
with your
writing !

Emily
McKay

MILLS & BOON®

First published in Great Britain 2006
Harlequin Mills & Boon Limited,
Eton House, 18-24 Paradise Road, Richmond, Surrey TW9 1SR

© Emily McKay 2006

ISBN-13: 978 0 263 84995 0
ISBN-10:   0 263 84995 3

Set in Times Roman 10½ on 12 pt.
171-0806-53733

Printed and bound in Spain
by Litografia Rosés S.A., Barcelona

HER WILDEST DREAMS

To my good friend Michelle Butler.
Thanks for your input on the book and for
lending your name to the Butler Steam Vac.

CHAPTER ONE

UNREQUITED love was for silly, foolish girls. Which was just one of the reasons Jane Demeo was fairly certain what she felt for her boss, Reid Forester, *wasn't* unrequited love.

Unrequited lust? Maybe. Unrequited knee-weakening, heart-pounding, gut-churning attraction? Possibly. But definitely not unrequited love. Besides, Jane was neither silly nor foolish. Love? Nope.

Though she'd never quite pinned down exactly what emotion it was she felt for Reid, there was one thing of which she was certain—its unrequitedness.

Reid Forester was the kind of upstanding, well-respected, all around good guy who would never dream of having an affair with an employee.

She, it turned out, was not quite that moral and often dreamed of having an affair with him.

That was, in fact, exactly what she was doing while sitting in her cubicle at work, when Audrey, Reid's assistant, stuck her head around the corner and handed her a note.

"Wh-wh-what's this?" But by the time she forced out the question, Audrey was long gone.

Jane flipped open the fine linen card stock and read the message inside. "Need to see you ASAP re: the Butler account. ~ R. Forester"

Jane's heart pounded as she read the tight masculine script. Reid needed to see her. Her.

She rolled her chair back to glance into the next cubicle where Teresa, the other member of her team, was putting the final touches on the ad they'd present at ten o'clock.

Why had Reid asked to see only her?

She glanced at the note clutched in her hand. Yep. That was definitely her name on the front. And, yep, that was definitely "ASAP."

Jane bumped her chair back, stood on trembling legs, and made her way down the hall to Reid's corner office. As she was waved into his office by Audrey her heart seemed to throw itself against her rib cage like a wild beast desperate to break free. Maybe it was fear. Maybe anticipation. Or maybe just the awareness that she'd never been alone with him before.

He stood with his back to her, staring out the floor-to-ceiling windows at the view of the Texas Capitol. Hands shoved deep into his pockets stretched the fabric of his white shirt taut across the impressive muscles of his back. From across the room, she felt the tension in his shoulders. Even alone, Reid didn't let down his guard.

Since he couldn't see her enter, she cleared her throat. Still he didn't turn around, but said, "Why don't you close the door behind you, Jane?"

He phrased it like a suggestion, but she recognized it for the order it was. The click of the latch seemed to echo in the silence that stretched between them, and her heart pounded until she was sure he must be able to hear it.

"You're wondering why I asked you here."

She nodded, then realized he couldn't see her. Praying she could keep her blasted stutter under control, she kept her answer short. "Yes."

Please don't say you called me here to fire me.

"Relax. I'm not going to fire you."

"How did—" she started to ask.

"You look ready to faint."

Only then did she realize that he wasn't looking out the window, but at her reflection in the glass. The floor seemed to tilt out from under her. She sucked in a deep breath, but the extra oxygen only made her feel more light-headed.

Though she could see him clearly in the window, his expression was guarded. Beside his reflection, she saw her own—all straight brown hair and wide eyes. She did indeed look ready to faint.

Suddenly he turned to face her. "I don't want you to be afraid of me."

Sensing he wanted a response, she said simply, "I'm not afraid of you." And for the first time in her life, speaking came easily to her.

His gaze moved over her face as if searching for the lie to her words. "I've tried to stay away."

"Stay away?" Though in her heart, she knew what he meant. He felt it, too. This magnetic pull between them.

He rounded the desk and crossed the room with impatient steps. He cradled her jaw in his palm, his thumb brushing her cheek. "No matter how I tell myself it's wrong, no matter how I try to stay away, it's no use." His thumb caught on her lower lip, tugging gently against her defenses.

Her breath came in bursts as heat spiraled through her body. The scent of his cologne—something woodsy and rugged—washed over her. She'd never been this close to him before and she had to tilt her head in order to look into his eyes. Eyes of pure green, without a fleck of gold or brown.

She only had to sway to press her body against his, yet somehow she resisted. She wanted this moment to be perfect. To last forever.

Just as Reid started to lower his mouth to hers she stopped him. "Wait."

His gazed clouded over with confusion and desire. "What?"

"You hardly know me," she protested. "You never even speak to me. I didn't think you even knew I existed."

"How could I not know you?" He cradled her face in both hands to gaze deeply into her eyes. "I've tried to ignore you. To ignore this. I haven't spoken to you because I've been afraid of giving in. I know it's wrong, but I can't stay away from you. You make me weak."

Perfect. Absolutely perfect.

Her body swayed towards his and she steadied herself by reaching for his arms. His biceps tightened as she wrapped her fingers around the hardened muscles, reminding her of his strength and power.

Yet she made him weak.

The thought sent a surge of feminine satisfaction through her. Why was she resisting this? She wanted him. Had wanted him from the moment she'd first seen him five years ago. And this moment was perfect.

As she tilted her mouth up to his her eyes drifted closed and she waited for his kiss…

"Damn it, Jane, you haven't fallen asleep, have you?"

Jane's eyes snapped open, a moment of foggy confusion evaporating as the real world shattered her fantasy.

Teresa's critical voice rang in her ears, effectively clearing her vision. She sprang from her office chair and turned to face Teresa, who, despite her diminutive size, managed to loom in the entry of Jane's cubicle.

"I w-w-wasn't—" Her words clogged in her throat, trapped by her desperation to explain. She forced herself to slow down, to draw in a calming breath. "I was just meditat—"

Teresa snorted, too impatient with Jane's verbal stumbling. "Meditate all you want, you know you'll still be a wreck at the presentation. Which, by the way, is in about ten minutes. Don't be late."

Teresa spun on her heel, trotting off towards the conference room, leaving Jane standing dumbfounded, embarrassment burning her cheeks, shame burning in her gut.

Damn it. Why did her tongue always trip her up? Just once, why couldn't she be ready with a snappy comeback? Why did her stutter always get the best of her?

Well, she wouldn't let Teresa keep the upper hand. Jane grabbed the black folio from her desktop and followed.

When they reached the conference room, she held out the oversized portfolio to Teresa. "My new idea for the ad."

Teresa's gaze flickered dismissively. "What's the point? We're meeting Reid and Matt now to show them our ideas for the Butler Steam Vac account. Even if this brainstorm of yours is better than what we've been working on, we don't have time to rework the pitch."

"We're not pitching to Butler until Friday, that's plenty of time. Besides, w-w-what we've got now is hackneyed. Y-you said so yourself yesterday. Frazzled mom steam-cleaning grape juice out of her carpet? It's been done. This new idea is s-s—"

"Is sexy. Yes, I know. Jane, all your ideas are sexy. But we're pitching an ad for a steam cleaner. I just don't see how that can be sexy."

"Just look at it?"

Teresa sighed, but took the portfolio from Jane. "I'll glance through it."

A few minutes later, while they waited for Reid and Matt Blake, the VP of Creative Development, Jane looked over Teresa's shoulder while she flipped through the sketches Jane had done the night before. Even though she'd mounted them on black paperboard mats, they were primitive. Normally, Pete, from the graphics department, would translate those ideas into a slick PowerPoint presentation. Today, there hadn't been time. Still, she was proud of her work.

This was her creativity—her mojo—at its absolute best. Another Reid-inspired fantasy turned into brilliant ad copy.

She'd had the idea late last night, while she sat on the floor of her living room dressed in her yoga pants and a tank top, sipping red wine out of a tumbler, staring at her empty fireplace, fantasizing. In her mind, she'd worn a flirty little black dress. The wine had been champagne. Flames had flickered in the fireplace. And Reid had been there.

As the fantasy had played out in her mind, she'd grabbed a notepad and started sketching.

A pair of champagne flutes discarded on the fireplace mantel. A faceless couple slow-dancing, their bare feet shuffling across plush carpet. Pan back to a shot of them on the floor, his hands braced on either side of her face as he leans in to kiss her, her knees bent, her thighs cradling him. Her toes curling into the carpet as her hips rock up to meet him. Pan away from the couple, past the champagne flutes to the Butler Steam Vac propped in the corner. Then the tagline, "Because sometimes you want your carpet to be really clean."

Jane held her breath as Teresa studied the last sketch. She thought she might even have heard a soft chuckle escape.

"W-w-well?" She lowered herself to the chair beside Teresa and scooted it up to the conference table.

Teresa narrowed her gaze to nearly a glare. "You know, it's good. You wouldn't have brought it in otherwise."

"But?"

"But… We present in—" she glanced at her watch "—less than five minutes. I'm not going to pull a fully developed pitch for a couple sketches. What we have is solid, too."

What they had had been done a thousand times. "But—"

"No." Teresa snapped the portfolio closed. "Look, Jane, it's my decision to make. When you're heading up your own team, you can make your own decisions. Until then, leave this kind of thing to me."

Jane nearly groaned in frustration. It always came back to that: Teresa's position as team leader.

Not that Jane couldn't be a team leader if she wanted to. Matt had offered to put her in charge of her own team more times than she could count. Lately, she'd been tempted to take him up on his offer. Sure, it was more money and more creative freedom. But it was also more work, more responsibility...and more of facing her gut-wrenching fear of giving presentations.

How could she accept a position as team leader when every time she opened her mouth her fear of stuttering crippled her into mute silence?

The answer was simple. She couldn't.

But she could fight for this idea. Especially since she knew she was right. "Teresa, w-w-we—"

But—once again—Teresa didn't even let her finish. "What we show Reid and Matt today has to be flawless. You and I both know how important this presentation is."

"We do?"

"Oh, Jane..." Teresa clucked patronizingly. "Forester+Blake has lost three major accounts in the past six months. They're looking for excuses to lay people off."

"Okay, th-then—" Jane drew in a shaky breath "—that's all the more reason to show Reid and Matt my new idea. It's much bet—"

"No. And that's my final word."

Before she could protest further, the door to the conference room swung open. Reid stood in the open doorway, turned in profile as he spoke to someone out in the hall.

He always dressed impeccably. Today he wore a slate-gray suit, a pale green oxford shirt that set off his eyes, and one of his cartoon ties. Marvin the Martian today, which was who he always wore for pitch meetings. He had one hand tucked into the pocket of his pants with his jacket caught behind his arm. Very *GQ*. Very unconsciously masculine.

She felt a shiver of anticipation cross her skin that she knew had nothing to do with the way he dressed. It wasn't his wealth or his position of power that got to her. It wasn't even those piercing green eyes of his.

The thing about Reid Forester that made her ache was the sense of barely restrained energy. Every time he walked into a room, she felt as if the room's center of gravity shifted. As if the sheer intensity of his personality pulled her inexorably towards him.

Then he turned to face her, meeting her gaze across the conference table. In an instant, the debate with Teresa, all her resentment about Teresa's dismissal of her ideas, and her fears about job security simply vanished. She felt nothing but that magnetic tug.

Jane tightened her grip on the chair, a half-hearted attempt to maintain her balance as the world tilted beneath her feet.

Reid nodded, smiling in greeting—that little half-smile of his, which always seemed both confident and wry. Desire wound its way through her stomach, making her blood pound and her breath come in ragged bursts. Just as if she were reliving the kiss she'd merely imagined.

She had only to close her eyes to feel his hands on her arms, pulling her to him. To feel his mouth pressed to hers. To feel his kiss, hot and needy. A little rough. A little desperate. A little…

…completely in her head!

Snap out of it, she mentally ordered.

But it was too late. Everyone in the room was staring at her expectantly.

Someone must have asked her a question, but she had no idea what it was. Once again, she'd been lost in her own little world. Spinning outrageous fantasies about her boss, completely unaware of what was going on around her.

Humiliation burned in her cheeks, almost—but not quite—knocking down the arousal that still gripped her body. She opened her mouth to speak. A hundred responses raced through her mind, but when she opened her mouth to say something—anything!—all that came out was a nervous squeak.

Great. Now, he undoubtedly thought she was just deranged. Brilliant.

Teresa, who was well acquainted with the effects of the stutter, gestured for everyone to sit with a sophisticated tinkle of laughter—that didn't sound at all deranged— then murmured, "Shall we just get started, then?"

Even though she'd seen Teresa do it a thousand times before, Jane still found Teresa's ability to command attention awe-inspiring.

Shoulders back, chin up, and confident smile firmly in place, Teresa effortlessly smoothed things over. She stepped forward, hand extended to Matt.

Following Teresa's lead, Jane shook his hand as well, but her own smile felt stiff and icy on her face, like a damp towel left to harden in the freezer.

Before she backed out of range, Reid stepped forward, also, his hand extended. She swallowed hard, hoping he wouldn't notice that her hand trembled as she slipped it into his.

"Nice to see you again, Jane."

Her gaze darted up to his face. He smiled at her and winked, undoubtedly trying to put her at ease. His attentions had the opposite effect.

His hand felt warm and strong around hers. She was intensely aware of the calluses on his palm—probably from the rock climbing he was rumored to do on the weekends. As he released her hand she felt his gold Texas A&M class ring brush against her fingers.

For an instant, the feel of his ring sent a shiver of alarm through her. Just how detailed had her drawings been? She'd sketched out her ideas so quickly, she couldn't remember any exact details. But she definitely remembered sketching an A&M ring.

She brushed aside her concerns. What did it really matter if Reid's ring was in the drawings? Bits and pieces of Reid had been showing up in her drawings for years. No one had ever noticed them.

"We're looking forward to seeing what you've come up with," Matt was saying when Jane forced her attention back to the meeting. "I talked to the people at Butler just this morning and assured them you're our most creative team."

Teresa smiled smugly. "Of course we are."

Matt rocked back in his chair with a laugh. "They just don't want to see another pitch about grape juice."

Teresa didn't even blanch. Without even an instant of hesitation, she snapped the laptop closed and reached for Jane's portfolio. "I've got just what they're looking for."

Jane watched, amazed, as Teresa seamlessly switched pitches. Should she be happy her idea had a shot, or irritated by Teresa's heavy-handedness? Did it matter? In the end, she did what she always did when Teresa gave presentations. She sat in silence, just glad she didn't have to do the talking.

A few minutes into the pitch, she hazarded a glance in Matt's direction. He was smiling and nodding his head, pleased with the ad idea, just as she'd known he would be. When she looked at Reid, however, her heart leapt into her throat. He'd leaned back in his chair, his elbow resting on the back of the empty chair beside him, his forefinger absently rubbing the stubble along his jaw. His posture was somehow both relaxed and coiled with energy.

She probably would have spent the rest of the meeting gazing at him if Audrey hadn't knocked on the door while Teresa was presenting the final drawing.

Audrey handed Teresa a phone message, then scurried away. Instantly, Jane knew something must be terribly wrong. Audrey wouldn't have interrupted the meeting otherwise.

As Teresa skimmed the note her face went white. She folded it neatly in half, no doubt trying to appear calm as she stood on legs that seemed to tremble.

For the first time since Jane had known her, Teresa's professional façade seemed to slip as she excused herself from the meeting and accepted Matt's reassurances that they could continue without her.

Almost as an afterthought, she turned to Jane. "You can finish up here?"

"Of course." She nodded, but Teresa was gone.

Jane turned back to Matt and Reid to find them watching her expectantly.

The two most important men in the company were

waiting for her to finish the presentation. Were waiting for her to talk.

Okay. She could do this.

Just finish the presentation, she ordered herself. *Don't think about Reid and Matt sitting there. Don't even look at them. Just concentrate on the picture.*

"As y-y-y—" But the words clogged in her throat like trees caught in a logjam.

Just a few short sentences. Just wrap it up. You can do this.

This time, when she opened her mouth, not even one word passed her lips. The logs caught, piling one upon another.

Just say the words, damn it. Just speak.

But whatever words she might have spoken finally splintered under the pressure. And suddenly the voice she heard in her head wasn't her own, but her mother's. *You're gaping like a fish. If you can't speak, close your mouth.*

Jane snapped her mouth shut as failure closed like a fist around her heart.

She tore her gaze away from her drawing to find Matt had rounded the conference table. He placed a comforting hand on her shoulder. "Don't worry. I think we've seen enough to approve the ad. It's good work."

Reid nodded, but didn't meet her gaze. "Excellent work."

Humiliation burned through her as she watched them leave. That was what she hated the most. The pity.

Don't be so hard on yourself. They liked the idea. Her idea. The team at Butler would love it, too. She just knew they would.

Eager to share the good news—and to make sure Teresa was okay—Jane left the conference room and went in search of her team leader. She found Teresa in the women's restroom carefully wiping away a mascara trail with a dampened paper towel.

Jane immediately rushed to her side. "What's wrong?"

"It's Noah. The school nurse called. She thinks it's appendicitis." Even her obvious embarrassment at being caught crying at work couldn't hide her underlying fear. "Look at me. I'm a mess. She assured me it's probably not that big a deal, but she still wants me to take him straight to the doctor. He'll probably be fine. It's just—"

It's just that Noah was Teresa's only child. And since her divorce three years ago, any time Noah got sick, the burden of caring for him rested solely on Teresa's shoulders.

"You don't have to explain," Jane reassured her.

"Thanks." Teresa drew in a shaky breath. "I'm on my way right now. Walk out with me and you can tell me how it went. They loved it, right?"

"I m-made a fool of myself, but they loved it." Unsure how to treat a crying Teresa, Jane ran her hand up and down Teresa's arm to comfort her. "What about you? Will you be okay?"

"I'll be better once I've seen him. Appendicitis just seems so scary. If he has to have it removed it'll be his first surgery. And I'll have to miss work. So before I go pick him up, I'll have to clear the time with Audrey and talk to Matt to see if he can do the Butler presentation."

Jane made the decision in an instant and the words were out of her mouth before she could give it more thought. "I'll talk to Matt about the presentation. Just let Audrey know you'll be out and head for Noah's school."

She didn't even stutter once when she said it, but she held her breath waiting for Teresa's response.

Teresa's face lit up. "Thanks, Jane. You're a doll."

As she watched Teresa rush for the door Jane told herself she hadn't lied. Not really. She would talk to Matt. She just wouldn't ask him to do the presentation for her.

She was going to do the presentation herself. She was tired of standing in the background. Tired of letting Teresa get all the credit for her good ideas. Most of all, she was tired of letting her stutter control her life.

CHAPTER TWO

"HERE's that file you asked for." Audrey, Reid's assistant, handed him a manila folder. "Will you need anything else before I go, sir?"

She stood on the other side of his desk, her hands folded primly in front of her.

"No, thank you, Audrey. You can go." He had to force himself to say it without smiling. Audrey took her job very seriously. And—despite her piercings and the tattoo of a phoenix scrawled up the back of her neck—seemed to have learned all her administrative-assistant skills from watching movies dating back to the early sixties.

She was always efficient, always unobtrusive and always offered to make his coffee, which he let her do since he'd hired her straight out of one of the espresso bars downtown.

"One more thing, Audrey."

Audrey was almost out the door when he stopped her. "Yes, sir?"

"Am I scary?"

Her eyebrows shot up. "Excuse me?"

"Do I scare people?"

"I…" Audrey bit down on her lip, gnawing on it for

a moment before saying, "I'm not sure I understand the question."

"Today in a meeting I noticed that one of my employees seems afraid of me." He didn't mention Jane by name. Audrey, for all her virtues at the coffee machine, liked to gossip.

"Do you want me to talk to the employee's supervisor?"

"No. No, that's not what I meant. Never mind. Forget it."

This time, he let Audrey leave. Alone in his office, he stared unseeing at the financial reports his CFO had foisted off on him that morning. Barely aware he was doing it, he tapped his fingers against the papers strewn over his desk. He leaned back in his chair, absently rubbing his jaw with his other hand as he stared into space.

He thought about what he knew of Jane. Long brown hair that looked surprisingly silky. Brown eyes that were a little too large for her heart-shaped face, and pale skin that looked as if it had rarely been touched by the sun and never by makeup. She usually wore unflattering, sack-like dresses, which didn't even hint at what her body might be like underneath. For all appearances, she was twenty-seven going on eighty-seven.

But appearances—he knew—could be deceiving. He'd bet almost anything the sexy concept for the new Butler ad had come straight out of her nondescript little head.

In the six years she'd been with Forester+Blake, he'd seen it time and again. The ideas from her team were always stylish, sexy and original. And they came from Jane. Teresa succeeded through hard work, charm, and sheer dogged persistence. Not creativity.

Jane, on the other hand, was bright, innovative,

and had a wicked sense of humor. Of course, he knew all of this secondhand, through other employees and through the copy she wrote. Around him, she was pallid, often mute, and generally terrified. He honestly couldn't remember if she'd ever even spoken to him.

Before he could give Jane any more thought, Matt rapped on the door frame and stuck his head in. "Working late again?"

"When am I not?"

Matt chuckled. "You work too hard."

"What's that supposed to mean?"

Matt had been his father's protégé. Portly, with graying hair and a full beard, to Reid, Matt had always seemed like a kindly elf. But the Papa Smurf-like exterior hid a keen intellect. "Go home. Get some rest. Relax a little bit."

"Relax? How am I supposed to relax with this hanging over my head?" He held up the financial report he'd been reading.

Matt shrugged. "So, money is tight. It's been tight before. It'll be tight again. It's the nature of the business."

"Come on, Matt. This isn't just the normal fluctuation that comes with a rough economy and you know it. If we don't get a new account—a big account— soon, we'll have to lay people off. Lots of people."

Matt's normal good humor faded a bit, but he didn't deny it. "Maybe we will. It happens sometimes."

He knew Matt was right. In the ad business, layoffs happened. If you lost a big account and didn't get another, suddenly half your employees had nothing to work on. But in the years he'd been running Forester+Blake, he'd managed to avoid them. So far.

Tightening his resolve, Reid shook his head. "I know you're right." He tapped the center of the file on his desk with his forefinger. "But if we can just—"

With uncharacteristic brusqueness, Matt interrupted him. "You know what your problem is, Reid?"

Reid was too surprised by Matt's question to respond with anything other than, "No. What?"

"You take this all too seriously." Reid tried to protest, but Matt didn't give him the chance. "No, hear me out. When you took over your father's job after he died, we all thought you did the right thing. Finally lived up to your responsibilities."

Reid accepted the compliment with a nod. "Thank you."

"We were wrong."

"Huh?"

"Look, Reid, this is a job, not jail time."

"What are you talking about?"

"You see this job—this company—as an obligation. Something you owe your parents for taking you in."

"No, I don't. I love this company."

"No. You loved your father. That's admirable. But you feel indebted to him. And you think running Forester+Blake will somehow pay him back."

"That's ridiculous."

"I don't think so. If you want to fill your father's shoes you're going to have to find a way to have a little more fun here. Your father loved this job. He loved this business. He didn't treat it like a chore."

Reid rocked back in his chair. "Are you telling me we're losing accounts because I'm not having enough *fun* at work?"

Matt shook his head ruefully. "Look, take it

however you want. Whether business is good or bad isn't the point."

"Then what is?"

"The point is, you're working yourself to death here. If you don't find something to enjoy in this job you're going to make yourself crazy. You'll burn out and end up hating this company. That's the last thing your father would have wanted."

Annoyed by Matt's assessment, he said, "My father wouldn't have wanted us to lose money, either."

"Would it help if I told you *Trés Bien* is looking for new representation?"

"*Trés Bien*?" He searched his mind for a minute before making the connection. "The women's lingerie store?"

"*Trés Bien*, the very lucrative lingerie store."

He raised his eyebrows and let out a low whistle. "A little out of our league, isn't it?"

"Not necessarily. From what I hear, they're looking for a fresh approach." Matt flashed him an impish smile. "Fresh approaches are what we do best."

"We're a lot smaller than whoever they've been working with," Reid pointed out. "Will they even talk to us?"

"One of your father's buddies from college works in their marketing department. If you fly out there at the weekend, I think you can woo him into getting us the meeting."

A meeting with *Trés Bien*?

Every mall in the country had a *Trés Bien*. Landing this account would make all the difference. No financial disaster. No layoffs. No guilt about running his father's business into the ground.

If they could just—

Once again, Matt interrupted his train of thought. "You know what I think?"

"I don't think I want to," Reid muttered.

"I think you should work on this yourself. I know, until now, I've always worked closely with the creatives and you've handled the financial end of things, but, let's face it, working with people is a lot more fun than working with numbers. You never know, you might actually enjoy your job." Matt didn't give him a chance to voice a denial before changing the subject. "By the way, you've heard about Teresa, right?"

"Teresa?"

"Yeah, her kid has appendicitis. She'll be out all week. Maybe longer."

Reid swallowed a groan of frustration. "Which means one of us will have to do the presentation at Butler."

"Actually, Jane's offered to do it."

"Jane?" Jane, who had barely squeaked out a word this afternoon, giving a make-it-or-break-it presentation?

Matt chuckled. "Don't worry. I'll go with her. I think this'll be good for her. She's ready for more responsibility, but sometimes gets a little intimidated. Besides, you'll need to get ready for your trip to New York."

Matt turned to leave, but Reid stopped him before he made it out the door. "Wait, one more thing."

"Shoot."

"Are people afraid of me?"

Matt raised his eyebrows. "Afraid of you? Who?"

"No one in particular. I was just curious."

"Not that I know of. But Angela thinks you scowl too much. And she wants you to come to dinner on your birthday."

"I'll think about it. But only if she doesn't try to set me up again."

"I'll pass along the message, but I can't promise she'll listen."

All alone in his office, he contemplated Matt's words. He'd been right about one thing: Reid didn't enjoy his job. Never had. He loved the company, if not the work. That would be enough.

Of course, Matt wanted him to work with the creatives, something Reid had avoided until now. For that matter, he didn't work closely with anyone other than Matt.

Being buddies with everyone at work might be more fun, but having fun wasn't his job. Running the company was. And emotional attachments to his employees would only make his job harder. When the time came to make tough decisions, he needed to be able to do what was right for the company, without letting his emotions get involved.

However, as much as he tried to maintain a certain distance between himself and his employees, this thing with Jane didn't sit right with him.

He certainly never meant to terrify anyone. He just didn't want to care more about their welfare than about the company. Besides, none of his father's employees had been afraid of him.

Shoving aside thoughts of his conversation with Matt, he reached for the creative file for the Butler account. He often looked over the work presented by his employees, but his interest was usually more professional than personal. Something about Jane just didn't fit. She was a mystery he couldn't ignore.

He opened the file, then turned it ninety degrees to look at the pictures inside. He flipped through them,

scanning each one before going back to the beginning
to study them in more detail.

On the fourth page, something caught his attention.
Just there, in the close-up of a man's hand pressed into
the carpet beside the woman's head. A lock of hair
curled over his fingers to end just beside a heavy ring.
Any native Texan would recognize the distinctive class
ring worn by everyone who graduated from Texas
A&M University.

He glanced down at his right hand, where he wore
his own chunky gold Aggie ring. About two inches
down, a faint scar slashed across his skin. He'd been
eleven when he'd gotten that scar from a fight outside
school where the other kid had pulled a knife.

Two days later, after stitches and a trip to the police
station, the family he'd been fostered with at the time
had sent him back to the group home, where he'd lived
for nearly three years before the Foresters had taken
him home when he was fourteen.

That scar had cost him a place with a nice family.
That scar was proof he couldn't stay out of trouble even
when it was in his own best interest. For years, he'd
hated that scar. Then, the Foresters had taken him in,
adopted him well past the age boys like him were ever
adopted, and for the first time in his life he'd had
security and stability.

Getting in that fight had been a stupid, reckless thing
to do. He worked hard now to control those rash
impulses of his. Mostly, he succeeded. Still, the scar was
a constant reminder of just how much he had to lose.

The scar had faded almost completely in the
twenty-one years since that fight. Most people didn't
even notice it. But apparently Jane was very observant.

Because the hand in the picture bore a scar nearly identical to his. Oh, she'd gotten the angle of it wrong. But that was definitely his scar, two inches below his Aggie ring, on his hand. Right there in the picture.

She wasn't afraid of him. She had a crush on him.

CHAPTER THREE

"ARE you crazy?"

Jane glared at her best friend, Jack Keegan, as he sat sprawled on her sofa, his boots propped on her coffee table, the neck of a Shiner Bock clenched between his fingers.

"No, I'm not crazy." She didn't bother to hide her exasperation. "I asked both of you here because I need your help."

She fixed what she hoped was a steady gaze on first Keegan and then Dorothea, the other half of "both of you". Her two friends couldn't be more opposite, but she hoped between the two of them they could muster up some decent advice.

She'd known Keegan since college, but she and Dorothea had been like soul mates ever since they'd met just a few years ago. Very odd soul mates, since Jane was a twenty-seven-year-old urban professional and Dorothea was a seventy-eight-year-old aging movie starlet. But they had a lot in common, since they both loved movies and volunteered at the Austin Animal Shelter. Jane only hoped that one of the things they didn't share was a sense of impending career-related doom.

Jane looked hopefully at Dorothea. "What do you think?"

"Let me consider…" Dorothea spoke slowly, each word pronounced with a stage actress's care as she sat perched on the edge of a wingback chair, a martini—very dry—in one hand while she stroked the cat on her lap with the other. The cat, Sasha, was a gorgeous silver tabby Jane was fostering from the animal shelter. "The presentation is on Friday?"

"Yes."

"And Teresa took off work this afternoon?"

"Yes."

"Remind me again why someone else can't do the presentation for you."

Before Jane could answer, Keegan held up his hand. "I got this one." He twisted on the sofa to face Dorothea. "'Cause if she can do this presentation, then she'll prove to herself that she can ditch Teresa, head up her own team, and generally look like a genius. Of course, if she fails, they could lose the account." Shaking his head he turned his attention back to Jane. "Which wouldn't be good for your career in today's competitive market."

"Th-thanks, Keegan, that's very helpful."

"No problem, doll." Keegan winked salaciously.

Dorothea issued a thoughtful, "Hmm," as she continued to pet Sasha, which Jane couldn't help resenting a little, since the temperamental cat never allowed her to even get within petting distance.

Keegan took another gulp of his beer and said, "What I don't get is why you're so afraid of freezing up during the presentation."

"Because of my stu—"

"Yeah, right. Your stutter. But what's the big deal,

really? So you stutter a little bit. As long as you don't freeze up—"

"But I do freeze up. All the time."

"Not all the time." Dorothea interrupted them. "At the animal shelter, I see you talking to strangers all the time. You can convince anyone who walks in to adopt a cat. Yes, sometimes you stutter while you're talking with them. But you never freeze up. Why is this situation at work any different?"

"It just is." She opened her mouth, trying to find the words to explain, but they simply weren't there.

The animal shelter was her haven. A place she felt completely comfortable. And completely determined to succeed.

But even more important, when she was talking to a stranger about a cat, she wasn't the center of attention. It wasn't about her. It was about the cat.

But an ad pitch meeting was completely different. With a pitch presentation she'd done, that was *her* up there on the screen. Her ideas. Her very soul. It made her feel so vulnerable.

That was why she froze up.

Or rather, why she'd frozen up in the past. This would be different. It had to be.

"But I can do this, right?" Jane prodded.

Dorothea's sharp gaze cut to hers. "You want to know if you can overcome your stutter long enough to give an important presentation? And your job is at stake if you don't succeed?"

"Y-yes," she said, far more boldly than she felt.

"Oh, man." Keegan chuckled. "You are so screwed."

She glared at him. "Could you at least try to be helpful?"

He yanked his feet off her coffee table and leaned forward, bracing his hands on his knees. "You want my advice?"

"Yes. But only if it's something more helpful than 'Are y-you crazy?' and 'Y-you are so screwed'."

"Okay, here's my advice. Don't do it."

"I w-was looking for something a little more productive than that. Maybe something a little more professional. I mean, weren't y-you a speech therapy major for a semester?"

Keegan stretched out his legs again. "Honey, I was a lot of majors for a semester."

Resisting the urge to shake him by the shoulders, she all but yelled, "Then, be helpful. I don't get what is wr-wr-wrong with y-you. For y-years you've been telling me to do something about Teresa. And now that I am, y-you're acting like a total ass."

Keegan's eyes narrowed and his cavalier attitude vanished. "Maybe I'm just not sure you're doing this for the right reasons."

"Wh-what's that supposed to mean?"

"Are you doing this for your career or are you doing this to impress Reid?"

Dorothea interrupted them by clearing her throat dramatically. As soon as she had their attention, she pronounced, "Marion Davies!" When Jane and Keegan merely stared blankly at her, Dorothea smiled broadly. "I've got it. I know how to help you."

"You do?"

"I do." Dorothea practically beamed. "It's Marion Davies."

Jane shot Keegan a confused look. "Who?"

"The actress," Dorothea supplied. "Marion Davies. She's the key."

"Wasn't she William Randolph Hearst's mistress?" Keegan asked.

"Oh, she was so much more than that! She was one of the most talented actresses of the time. A true comedic genius and great lady. I met her once, you know. Just as kind and generous as—"

"What's this have to do with Jane?" Keegan asked, cutting Dorothea off.

"Why, everything. Don't you see? Marion Davies spoke with a stutter. In the golden age of silent films, her stutter was never an issue. But, when talkies came out, everyone feared her career would be over."

Jane's heart tightened with compassion. She could imagine Marion's plight only too well.

"So what happened?" she asked.

"In nineteen twenty-nine, Marion starred in her first talkie, *Marianne*. She sang, she danced, she even spoke with an accent. And she never stuttered once. You see, Marion Davies stuttered, but her character Marianne did not."

"So what you're saying is—"

"All you have to do is create a character to play. An alternate persona, if you will. One who doesn't stutter."

Jane felt her breath catch in her throat. Could it really be that simple? Could this really be the answer, after years of stuttering, of awkward silences and pitying glances, of avoiding words she thought might trip her up?

But—

Keegan snorted loudly. "This is the stupidest idea I've ever heard."

Dorothea shot him a smug, sly smile. "You just don't like it because you didn't think of it."

"No." He shook his head. "I don't like it, 'cause it doesn't make any sense. The idea is for Jane to impress these bigwigs at work, right? But if she gives this presentation dressed up as some alternate persona then nothing has changed. If people don't know it's her doing the presentation, then Jane still isn't getting credit for her work. Besides, won't the people at Butler be confused when Jane comes to give the presentation dressed up like some person who doesn't even work for Forester+Blake?"

As Keegan ticked off each of his objections on his fingers, Jane looked to Dorothea for answers. Dorothea merely chuckled, patting Keegan's hand reassuringly.

"Oh, you silly boy, you've misunderstood me completely. Of course we want Jane to get credit for her ideas. I'm not suggesting she try to fool other people into thinking she's a different person. She only has to fool herself. Her persona will be all up here." Dorothea tapped her temple. "If she believes she's not going to stutter, then she won't."

"Sure, I guess." Jane didn't even bother to try to sound more confident than she felt.

Dorothea's heavily made-up face beamed with anticipation. "Of course, you'll need a new haircut. New clothes. A whole new look, I believe."

Keegan rose and headed for the door. "If y'all are going to talk about clothes, I'm outta here."

Jane frowned as she watched him leave. What was up with him?

Before she could give it any more thought, Dorothea carefully deposited Sasha on the floor, then pulled Jane into the hall bathroom to face the mirror. Sasha followed, mewing indignantly over her mistreatment.

As Dorothea ran an arthritic hand through Jane's long hair she murmured, "Something short, I think. And blonde."

"Blonde?" Jane squeaked.

Instead of answering, Dorothea grabbed a handful of fabric from the back of Jane's shirt, bunching the fabric so it stretched taut across the front. "And some decent clothes to show off your marvelous figure."

"What's wrong with my clothes?"

"Darling, life's too short to wear such ugly clothing. Besides, you need a costume to help you get into character."

Jane eyed Dorothea warily. "Why do I suspect this 'costume' will involve a lot of skimpy clothes I normally wouldn't be caught dead in?"

Dorothea quirked one elegantly penciled-in eyebrow. "This presentation, you're giving it to men, correct?"

"Yes."

"Men are hardwired to respond to short skirts and low-cut dresses. Why not use that to your advantage?"

Jane was pretty certain her stridently feminist mother could have come up with some excellent reasons why not. But Jane was about to face her deepest fear. She needed all the help she could get. Still…

"I don't know," she hedged.

"What's not to know? You have a gorgeous figure. Frankly, I'm appalled you haven't been using it to your advantage before now."

Jane frowned as she studied her reflection in the mirror. Funny, she'd always felt as if that "gorgeous figure" Dorothea was so impressed with didn't really fit her personality. It was simply too much. Too curvy. Too lush. And the few times in her life when she'd dressed to show it off, it had garnered her too much male attention.

Male attention in and of itself wasn't bad. But men had certain expectations of women built like her. They expected her to be flirty and charming. They expected sex-kitten personalities in sex-goddess bodies. But there was one thing she couldn't stand—the inevitable reaction.

Men wanted one thing, and what they got was her. A little quiet. A little shy. Even when her stutter didn't freeze her up completely, she tended to measure her words carefully. Men were inevitably disappointed.

She'd long ago tired of facing their disappointment.

Encouraged by Jane's silence, Dorothea blithely went on. "Of course, you still need to pick your persona. If you could be anyone in the world, who would it be?"

Sasha leapt to the counter, swishing her tail dramatically and forcing Jane's attention away from the nerve-racking prospect of life as a blonde.

As she watched, Sasha met her gaze in the mirror, practically hypnotizing Jane with her elegant blue eyes.

"Sasha," she said with sudden clarity.

"The cat?"

"Yes." Jane nodded, sure she'd found the perfect persona to emulate. "I want to be Sasha the cat."

As if she knew she was the topic of conversation, Sasha bumped her head against Jane's arm.

"Think about it," Jane said. "Everybody loves Sasha, but she doesn't give a damn about anyone. She's cool, confident, and in control of every situation."

Dorothea nodded. "I believe you're right. Sasha just might be the perfect persona for you."

Jane wanted desperately to believe it really was that simple. If she could overcome this fear of giving presentations, she wouldn't need Teresa anymore. She wouldn't have to worry about losing her job. Everyone at work would realize that her good ideas and her hard work were...well, *hers*.

She nearly laughed out at loud at her pathetic attempts at self-delusion. "Everyone at work." Right. That was who she was worried about. Her sudden desire for recognition didn't have anything to do with a certain sexy CEO. Not a thing.

Yep. That was denial at its best.

Okay, so maybe she was delusional about her reasons for wanting to give this presentation. The question was, was she delusional enough to fool herself into thinking she was someone else?

Dorothea was true to her word. By the time Jane walked through the doors of Forester+Blake two days later, she looked so different, no one recognized her.

The day before at the salon, Dorothea had directed the cutting and highlighting of her hair. Now, blonde waves hung to just below her jawline in a sexy tousle of curls. The style accentuated the delicacy of her chin and made her cheekbones seem more pronounced. A choppy fringe of bangs framed her eyes, making them appear wider and more prominent. She looked...if not gorgeous, then at least far more striking than she ever had before.

Her years of quietly slipping under everyone's radar were coming to an end. Sasha would never be overlooked.

However, she'd been unable to replicate the hairstyle

herself. So this morning Dorothea had arrived at her apartment to once again do her magic. As a result, Jane's scalp still stung from having her hair sculpted into place and her sinuses still twitched from the over-spray of too many products.

As she worked her way through the break room she noticed Pete, who did graphics for their team, making his morning latte at the espresso bar. He was chatting with some guy from Account Services as he waited for the machine to do its thing. He glanced in her direction, then did a noticeable double take.

At first, she merely laughed at his reaction. She still wasn't comfortable "in character", but it was too late to back out now. With that thought propelling her forward, she wove her way through the tables to the espresso bar. Pete glanced to either side—to make sure she really was waving at him—then straightened, puffing out his chest as he smiled at her.

That was when it hit her. Pete hadn't recognized her. Even after she waved and crossed the room to talk to him, he didn't put the pieces together.

She reached around him for a coffee mug. "Hi, Pete."

"Hi…"

He seemed to be struggling for a name, so she supplied one. "Jane."

"Jane?" His smile strained, but didn't disappear altogether.

"Jane," she repeated. The machine squealed as it finished squirting foam onto his latte, so she removed his cup and handed it to him. Being the center of his attention worked over her nerves, so that when she opened her mouth she felt the familiar stiffness tightening her throat. "Jane Demeo. We w-work together. My cubicle is next to y-yours. That Jane."

Finally his smile cracked under the strain. He squinted at her, blinking rapidly. "Jane! What'd you do to yourself?"

She shoved her mug under the espresso machine's spout and pushed a few buttons. "A friend gave me a makeover. She thought it'd give me more confidence at the pitch today. Do y-you think it'll help?" she asked playfully, but when she glanced over at Pete, he was gaping at her. When he didn't join in with her laughter, his attention made her shift uncomfortably. "Pete, close y-your mouth. It's rude to stare."

The machine sputtered out the last of her foam, and she snagged her mug, relieved to escape Pete's scrutiny. Unfortunately, Pete followed.

He caught up with her just outside the partition that separated their cubicles. He darted around her.

"Jane, I'm sorry. You just look really different."

Trying to hide how flustered she felt, she sighed as if exasperated by the delay. "Oh, for goodness' sake." Jane ducked under Pete's arm and into her cubicle.

This was not going as she'd hoped. Dorothea had sworn that this makeover would give her confidence. That a new haircut and a snazzy new outfit would complete her new persona.

Instead, they'd made her the center of attention. And it did not feel good. She had no more confidence than she'd had yesterday and her Sasha persona was nowhere to be seen.

Her new curls made her feel exposed, as did the outfit she'd borrowed from Dorothea—a short skirt and a double-breasted jacket. The skirt showed off her legs, the jacket nipped in at her waist, and showed way more of her cleavage than she ever wanted her colleagues to see.

Naturally, when she'd tried on the outfit, she'd protested. It was unprofessional. It was tacky. She'd probably catch a cold. But all her protestations had fallen on gleefully deaf ears. Dorothea had been thrilled. "Honey," she'd said, "with a body like this you don't need to look professional."

And if the way Pete was staring at her was any indication, Dorothea had been right.

Jane paused, her hand hovering over her keyboard. If Dorothea had been right about that, what else might she be right about?

Jane squeezed her eyes closed and tried to picture Sasha the cat. Her cool, silvery beauty. Her absolute confidence that everyone loved her. Her "you know you want to touch me, but don't you dare try it" attitude.

If Sasha could convey all that with a single glare from her ice-blue eyes, then surely Jane—with her college education and years of writing experience—could manage a simple sentence or two that would put Pete in his place.

Jane crossed one leg over the other, propped her elbows far back on the arms of her chair and spun around to face Pete. She was acutely aware that her skirt rode up far higher on her thigh than she was used to. She was equally aware that her posture displayed her breasts to their best advantage.

Though she'd never before used her body to get what she wanted, she knew Sasha would.

"Pete, be a doll and double-check the graphics. We can't afford to slip up on this."

Be a doll? Had she actually said that? She held her breath, waiting for him to laugh at her.

Instead, Pete nodded—without taking his eyes from her chest. The smile he sent her was a little dopey. "I'll get right on it."

Feeling baffled, she watched him leave. Was it really that easy? Could men really be won over with *faux* confidence and a low-cut blouse?

That was when it hit her. Just now, she hadn't stuttered when talking to Pete. She hadn't once felt her words stumble over themselves. Score one for Sasha the cat. Now if only her newfound confidence would hold through this afternoon's meeting. That would be the real test.

After all, Pete was easy. It was no great coup to snag the attention of a guy whose primary experience with women outside of work came from watching *The Real World* on MTV. The real test would come this afternoon when she had to fake her new confidence in front of the team from Butler.

Ever since he'd recognized himself in Jane's drawing, Reid hadn't been able to stop thinking about her. Since Monday, he'd gone back through her work for the past four years. He'd found references to himself in at least half a dozen of her ads.

In one, it was a pair of men's shoes discarded by his lover's bed—his shoes. In another, it was the cowlick on a man's head as he bent to kiss a woman—his cowlick. His brand of ballpoint pen scribbling a love letter. His briefcase. His car. His Aggie ring.

It was driving him crazy.

A week ago, she'd been just another employee.

Someone he barely knew. Now, she was all he thought about.

Studying her work had given him a glimpse into her mind. Slowly he was learning how she thought. And it intrigued him.

She'd come up with some pretty sexy stuff. And each time he caught sight of himself in one of her ads, it turned him on just a little bit more.

Which confused the hell out of him. He'd spent his entire professional career keeping his distance from his employees. Given the high turnover rate in advertising, he'd always thought that best. He hated the idea of firing anyone, let alone a friend.

So, he kept his distance. He never wanted to be their buddy or pal. He didn't hang out with them after work. He sure as hell didn't date any of them. Which meant he never would have looked twice at Jane. Of course, now that he knew what went on in that head of hers…

Now that he knew, he was in serious trouble. He'd been studying her. Walking by her desk in the middle of the day to see what she was wearing in hopes her clothes would hint at the body she kept hidden beneath her sack-like dresses. Making excuses to say hello or to chat with employees who had cubicles nearby.

He'd even taken to going to the break room several times a day to pick up coffee in hopes of running into Jane. In fact, he'd even been tempted to attend the Butler pitch meeting this afternoon, just so he could see her. Thank goodness, he'd talked himself out of that.

He scrubbed a hand down his face and stood to leave. This had to stop.

It didn't matter what she looked like under her clothes. It didn't matter how erotic her imagination was. It didn't even matter if he starred in every one of her sexiest fantasies.

She was an employee. Off limits. Forever.

Until she either quit or he fired her. He paused, giving it some thought.

"Yep, fire her," he muttered aloud as he grabbed his jacket from the coatrack by the door. "That'll drive her right into your arms."

Feeling too restless to go home and too edgy to go out, he went up to the roof to watch the sunset, something that always calmed his nerves.

Maybe once the sun went down he'd feel better. Maybe he'd grab a bite to eat on the way home. Maybe even at one of the pubs downtown where singles hung out. An evening of mindless sex would certainly take the edge off.

Unfortunately, it wasn't mindless sex that interested him.

CHAPTER FOUR

SASHA was a hit. The guys at Butler loved her and they adored the idea for the ad. Sasha had won the account, effectively securing Teresa's and Jane's jobs and practically guaranteeing Jane her own team during the reorganization. Matt had beamed with pride. Which was exactly what she wanted.

Wasn't it?

So why did she feel so blue? Was Keegan right, or could she just chalk up her funk to hunger and exhaustion?

At any rate, by the time Jane left the Butler headquarters and made it across town it was nearly eight. She still hadn't eaten and she still needed to stop by the office to drop off the laptop she'd borrowed for the presentation. She guided her car off Interstate 35 at the downtown exit and turned west towards the Capitol and The Prescott Towers where Forester+Blake had its offices.

The Prescott Towers were two twenty-story buildings in the heart of downtown Austin. The North Tower, which housed Forester+Blake and a host of other businesses, had a view of the state capitol grounds and the University of Texas campus. The South Tower, the

Prescott Hotel, from which the Towers got their name, looked down on Town Lake as it snaked through downtown. The Towers shared a ground-level lobby and atrium, complete with a handful of cafés, shops and a full-service business center.

The hotel's top floor was taken up with a five-star restaurant, The River City Grill, which overflowed up to the patio on the roof. But no one ever went up to the roof of the business tower.

Watching the hotel guests come and go through the lobby had always fascinated Jane. Not long after she'd been hired at Forester+Blake, Jane had made friends with one of the hotel's bellboys and talked him into giving her the full "behind the scenes" tour of the buildings. She'd seen the kitchens, the service elevators, and even the laundry chutes. While the view from the roof of the hotel was certainly impressive, her favorite spot in either of the buildings was the rooftop of the business tower where no one else ever went. A calm— if somewhat dingy—oasis from the bustle and pressures of the office. A haven in the otherwise frantic buildings.

On a Friday night, most of the shops in the lobby had already closed, but the restaurants would be open for a few more hours. Hunger got the better of her and she stopped to buy a sandwich and an iced tea before taking the elevator up to the tenth floor to drop off the laptop.

A few minutes later, she stood by her desk, the empty white paper bag discarded by her keyboard, the sandwich still wrapped in butcher paper. Funny, she didn't feel tired anymore. All alone in the empty offices, her take-out sandwich seemed a sad way to end such an important day. She would have gone to Keegan's to celebrate if he hadn't been acting so oddly lately. He obviously didn't approve of Jane's plan or of Sasha.

She dropped the Italian sub back in the bag, grabbed her iced tea and headed to the elevators. She got off at the nineteenth floor, then took the stairs up to the roof.

When the weather was nice, she came up here sometimes for lunch or just to think. Today would have been too hot, but the evening had brought a respite from the Indian summer and the breeze felt good against her bare legs and exposed neck.

Only the last gray streaks of dusk lingered in the west as she carefully made her way across the rooftop to the northeast corner and the best view of the Capitol, lit from hundreds of ground lights so that it gleamed nearly white. A long-abandoned wrought-iron table and chairs were the only evidence anyone else had ever come up here to enjoy the view and the solitude.

When she reached the table, she realized only one chair remained. She set down her tea and pulled her sandwich from the bag. Before she could sit, she heard a voice from the shadows.

"You missed the sunset."

She whirled towards the sound. Even with his face and form obscured by the darkness, she knew instantly that the voice belonged to Reid Forester.

When her eyes adjusted to the growing darkness, she made out his silhouette, seated in a chair, his elbows propped on his knees.

"I didn't mean to startle you. I'm sorry."

As he stood and walked towards her, she struggled

to think of something to say. Something brilliant. Something witty. Something that would come out smoothly without any embarrassing stumbling and stammering. But her words failed her, as they so often did.

"I-I thought I was alone," she muttered.

He stopped just at the other side of the table. In the half-light, his clothes were all shades of gray, but she could just make out the image of Spongebob Squarepants on his loosened tie.

When her gaze drifted back to his, she found him studying her. Heat flashed through her body in response. In the years she'd known him, he'd seen her hundreds of times, but he'd never really looked at her, never turned the full force of his attention solely to her. The sensation was more potent than she'd ever imagined.

That was saying a lot.

Her heart rate kicked up a notch and she found herself struggling to suck air into her lungs. Things like breathing and pumping blood were so much easier when he wasn't near.

How could a man look sexy when she could barely see him? Still, she could picture him—and she'd spent enough time studying him to do the image justice.

She could even sense the smile in his voice as he spoke. "I thought I was the only one who came up here."

Hoping to hide how much she wanted to melt into a puddle at his feet, she toyed with the straw of her iced tea. "I-I, um…b-bribed one of the bellboys. He said the best view of the Capitol was from up here," she admitted. Then she laughed awkwardly. "That seems strange, doesn't it?"

Her self-consciousness surprised Reid. In his experience, women with knockout figures like hers rarely felt self-conscious about anything. He couldn't make out her features, but the city lights beyond the rooftop clearly defined her silhouette.

Wanting to put her at ease, he said, "I won't tell anyone."

Despite himself, he couldn't stop staring at the woman who'd invaded the private spot he'd been coming to for years to be alone and think. Not that he minded the intrusion. Of all the hotel guests to wander up onto the roof...

The details of her face were indiscernible in the fading light, but he caught a hint of a plucky chin and a small, upturned nose. The backlighting made her hair appear as a halo of sexy jaw-length curls.

In fact, from the way she kept toying with her straw and glancing at him from under her lashes, she seemed more nervous-schoolgirl than sex goddess.

Intrigued, he held out his hand. "I'm Reid Forester."

She stiffened, her gaze darting to his face. He sensed her confusion as her whole body seemed to recoil from him. Had he misread her earlier friendliness?

He shoved his hand back in his pocket. "Well, then, I'll leave you to the view." He'd made it nearly to the door when her words stopped him.

"Don't go."

He turned to face her. The failing light that rendered her expression unreadable accentuated the curvy femininity of her figure.

"You seemed to want to be alone," he explained.

"I did. But—"

"But?"

"But now I think it might be nice to have you here, Mr. Forester."

Her voice caught on his name and he was struck again by the familiarity of her.

"Have you eaten?" She gestured towards the white paper bag. "If not, we could share my sandwich."

"Call me Reid. The only person who calls me Mr. Forester is my assistant."

A smile played at the corners of her lips. "Reid."

He imagined he heard a blush of embarrassment, but he knew it was a trick of the darkness. He could no more see the color of her cheeks than the color of her eyes.

"And you are…" he prodded.

She hesitated only a second before giving him her name. "Sasha."

This time, it was she who extended her hand to him. As he took it in his he felt that same twinge of familiarity—as if there was something about her that he should recognize.

However, that sensation was overwhelmed by the much stronger sense of awareness that washed over him. Awareness of her many contradictions. The delicacy of her hand, the firmness of her grasp. The luxurious scent of her perfume, the no-nonsense blunt cut of her nails. The way she let her hand linger in his, almost caressing his palm, then pulled away abruptly, as if embarrassed by the intimacy of their touch.

"Well, Sasha, I haven't eaten yet. There's a restaurant on the top floor of the hotel tower. We could grab something there."

She laughed, a husky little chuckle that tugged at something in his gut, even though she was so clearly laughing at him.

"What?" he demanded.

"That restaurant where you want to grab a bite is a fifty-dollars-a-plate kind of place."

He hadn't seen that coming. She dressed like a woman who ate at fifty-dollar-a-plate restaurants all the time. And the Prescott wasn't a cheap hotel. If she could afford to stay there, she could afford to eat wherever she wanted.

Still, it pleased him that she didn't prefer the stifling pretensions of The River City Grill. "So?"

"So..." she hemmed, as if she'd just realized she'd said the wrong thing "...you just don't seem like a River-City-Grill kind of guy."

Surely she couldn't see him any better than he could see her. So what had given him away? "What kind of guy do I seem like?"

"Maybe like a share-an-Italian-sub-on-the-roof kind of guy."

Something tightened deep within him at the teasing playfulness of her suggestion and he mentally conceded victory.

She was completely enticing. No woman had captured his attention so totally since...well, since Jane had on Monday.

This woman was nothing like Jane. And yet...and yet there was something familiar about her.

Oh, man. He had it bad.

Here he was with this gorgeous creature, who seemed to be interested in him, and he was trying to convince himself that she reminded him of Jane. Pathetic.

He couldn't have Jane. She was off limits. But there was no reason why he couldn't enjoy Sasha's company for a few hours.

As he walked back towards her he picked up the chair he'd been sitting on and dragged it closer to the table. She pulled the sandwich from the bag and he asked, "From the deli downstairs?" She nodded. "With hot or sweet peppers?"

"Both."

"Really? Not many people go for both."

"That's just the way I like it. Hot and sweet." She lingered over the words as if relishing their flavor.

Hot and sweet? Damn, he was in trouble.

He couldn't tell if she'd meant the *double entendre* or not. If she'd realized the sexual implication of her words before or after she'd said them.

"Is that right?" he asked. "So you've eaten there before?"

"Occasionally."

"Do you always stay at the Prescott when you're in town?"

She paused in the process of unwrapping the sandwich, then said, "Well, this sub shop is a chain. They have locations all over Texas."

"Is that right?"

"They have a couple of locations in Dallas."

After unwrapping the sub, she hesitated, clearly unsure how to divide it. He pulled out his pocketknife and, after wiping the blade clean on a napkin, sawed the sandwich in half. He moved the two halves to opposite corners of the butcher paper.

"Dallas? Is that where you're from?" he asked before taking a bite.

Instead of digging into the sandwich, she tore off a

corner of the bread and popped it into her mouth. "I grew up in Richardson, just north of Dallas."

"You're prevaricating."

"I'm not." But her protestation held a smile. "That's where I'm from."

"Is that where you live now?"

"Does it matter?" she asked before taking a bite.

"If I don't know where you live, how can I find you again?"

He said the words half in jest. However, she seemed to take him seriously. She pulled back sharply from her sandwich, leaving a dribble of hot pepper sauce on her lower lip. In a gesture so unconsciously erotic it made him ache, she dabbed at the sauce with her fingertip and then nudged the dribble into her mouth before sucking the remains from her finger.

His gut tightened. Her eyes met his, and she stilled, suddenly aware she'd held his attention. She stiffened, then jerked her hand away from her face. Self-consciously, she blotted her lips with her napkin.

After setting aside the half-eaten sandwich, she asked, "What makes you so sure you'll want to find me again after tonight?"

"A woman who watches sunsets from the roof and eats my favorite sandwich? You may be my soul mate."

She gave an exaggerated wince. "Ah, that's quite a pick-up line. You use it often?"

"Ouch."

She laughed and picked up her drink. "You'll survive."

"If you're trying to distract me, it's not working."

"Distract you from what?" she asked, her voice all mock innocence.

"From noticing that you still haven't told me where you live. Or what your last name is, for that matter."

"I just don't see the point," she admitted. She gestured to the sandwich, the rooftop, and the two of them. "This is nice. But I'm not foolish enough to think two strangers sharing a sandwich is anything more than what it is."

"Have dinner with me tomorrow. Then we won't be strangers. It'll be our first date."

She arched her eyebrow. "Our first date?"

"Or our second, depending on whether or not you want to count this one."

"That's a little optimistic of you. Tonight's not even over."

"Which means I have plenty of time to convince you."

"Maybe you should have waited. You may decide you don't want to see me again."

His gaze drifted over her face. Not that he could see much in the dark, but it was enough. She wasn't Jane. Thank God.

It was a such a relief to find himself attracted to a woman he could actually be with, he chuckled as he said, "That's not going to happen."

She tossed aside the remains of her sandwich and wiped her fingers on one of the napkins. She stood and reached for her purse.

"I should be going."

He felt a flash of panic. If he didn't stop her, she'd walk right out of his life and he'd never know who she was. He grabbed her wrist. "Don't."

She tugged her arm, but not firmly enough for him to believe she really wanted him to release her.

Her wrist felt small in his hand. Her bones delicate.

Her skin silken and smooth. He felt her pulse under his fingertips and his own pulse leapt to match hers as it pounded with awareness.

He forced himself to release her. "Don't go."

Her arm dropped to her side and she looked up at him from under her lashes. Humor and heat mixed in her gaze.

So that pounding pulse wasn't caused by fear, but by desire. The same as his.

"You only want me to stay because you think I won't."

There was a petulant quality to her voice. As if she wanted to be convinced. As if she wanted him to grovel.

Well, he wasn't going to beg. Not yet, anyway. "So, you think I'm like a child? I want only what I can't have?"

"No. But I do think if you had me, you'd be very disappointed with what you got." But the saucy tilt of her head and the mischievous tone of her voice said something else entirely.

He wouldn't be disappointed. Neither of them would be and they both knew it.

"You underestimate your effect on me."

"Perhaps you overestimate it."

"You're a remarkable woman, Sasha."

"On the contrary, I'm quite ordinary. Yesterday you would have passed me on the street without even noticing me," she teased. "And by tomorrow, you will have forgotten all about me."

"You're wrong. By tomorrow I'll be bribing the concierge to learn your full name."

"You're welcome to try." She might as well have double-dared him. "But it won't help you find me."

"But I will find you." He couldn't say why he was

so sure of himself, but he felt his conviction deep in his gut. He'd do whatever it took to find Sasha again.

What had started as gentle teasing had become much more. This was no longer simply a matter of passing the evening with a stranger. By refusing to give him her full name, she'd issued a challenge, one he intended to take her up on. Besides, he needed the distraction from Jane.

He followed behind her as she made her way to the stairwell that would take her back into the building. But instead of escaping down the stairs, she stopped.

An aluminum safety light hung over the door. She stood just outside the circle of light cast by its bulb.

"Please don't follow me." For the first time, she sounded serious. They were no longer playing.

"Give me a reason not to." She shook her head, but he ignored her. "Are you here with a husband? Is that why you won't see me again?"

It was a question he knew he had to ask, but it curdled his stomach.

Her eyebrows snapped together and she stiffened in indignation. "Of course not! If I were married, I certainly wouldn't be here with you."

Thank goodness.

Then another thought fell quickly after the last. "A fiancé? A boyfriend?"

"No. Neither."

"Then see me tomorrow night."

She frowned and her gaze darted away from his. She was wavering; he could sense it. He closed the distance between them. Though he ached to touch her, he didn't. He didn't want to scare her off.

So instead of pulling her into his arms, he braced

his hand on the wall beside the door. He inhaled the scent of her.

Beneath her expensive perfume, he caught a whiff of sandwich—the spicy pepper sauce, the oregano, and capicolla ham. And beneath that, something else. Something fruity and light. He leaned in closer; it was her hair. She washed her hair with apple-scented shampoo. Just one more fascinating contradiction. One more reason he couldn't let her go until he'd unraveled the mystery.

"I'll find you again either way, so you might as well agree. You've made yourself too intriguing for me to simply let you slip away."

She looked up at him, her eyes huge and startling in the light. "You're not going to make this easy, are you?"

"Not at all."

She sighed, a sound so annoyed...so petulant, he couldn't resist leaning down and pressing his lips to hers. To his surprise, her mouth opened immediately beneath his. Her lips were pliant. Soft and warm.

She tasted like the peppers from her sandwich, hot and sweet. Fiery and spicy, with a hint of honeyed compliance.

The heat from her kiss spilled over to fill his blood. The urge to deepen the kiss, to mold her body to his, to trap her against him pounded through his veins. He heard her moan, felt her hand flutter by his side, then land on his hip.

That simple touch broadcast her acquiescence. He'd won and that was enough. For now.

He was a breath away from ending the kiss when he felt her melt against him. Total surrender. Her body arched towards his and her hands clutched at his hips, then his arms, then buried in his hair. He angled his head to deepen the kiss but her mouth tore away from his as she moaned low in her throat.

The sound pulled at something deep inside of him, heightening his own arousal. In an instant, he went from merely wanting her to needing her. Passionately. Desperately. Immediately.

CHAPTER FIVE

"OH, REID."

He barely heard Sasha cry out over the pounding of his own blood.

"Wait."

He stilled instantly.

"We should—"

"Wait," he said, panting. Of course.

Of course they should wait. They'd just met. They were on a rooftop, for Pete's sake. Without a bed nearby. What had he planned on doing? Taking her up against the stairwell door?

Laboring to control his breath—not to mention his desire—he wrapped his arms around her and held her to his chest. "You're right. We should wait."

She leaned into him as if absorbing his strength. Which was ironic considering how unbelievably weak he felt around her.

"Meet me tomorrow night," he asked again. Begged was more like it.

"Yes."

Triumph surged through him at that simple word.

"Tomorrow night," she repeated. "In the lobby of the hotel."

"Tomorrow," he agreed. Then it hit him. The meeting with *Trés Bien* in New York. There was no way he could get out of it. "No, wait. Not tomorrow. I'll be out of town. I might be away all week. What about Friday? Will you still be here then?"

He held his breath, waiting for her answer. Maybe Matt could go to New York.

Even as the thought flickered through his mind, he knew it wasn't possible. He couldn't throw away a shot at the biggest account the company had ever had over a woman he'd just met.

Thankfully, he felt her nod against his chest. "I'll still be here."

Her arms tightened around his waist and he felt her sigh against his throat, inhaling deeply as she nuzzled his neck.

Suddenly, standing like that in the dark, with her in his arms, this all felt like much more than a playful bout of lust. More than desire heightened by curiosity.

This woman, with her compelling blend of sensuality and self-consciousness, with her beauty and quick wit, spoke to him as no other woman had. And holding her in his arms almost drove from his mind every other woman he'd ever known. Almost.

Even Sasha couldn't make him completely forget Jane, or the troublesome and inconvenient appeal she held for him.

But taking Sasha to bed would drive Jane from his mind. He was sure of it.

"Promise you'll meet me on Friday," he begged, now more desperate than ever.

"I—"

"Promise me," he said again.

Finally she nodded. "I'll meet you Friday. In the hotel lobby. But you have to promise not to follow me tonight."

"Done."

And like that, she was gone. She slipped through the door behind her and disappeared. He stood there for a long minute, hand still braced on the wall beside the door, head ducked, breathing deeply of the air still filled with her scent. Her complex, many-layered scent.

He gave her enough time to make it down a flight of stairs, and out into the hall, before grabbing his jacket from the ground and following her. He bypassed the elevator and used the stairs to go straight to the lobby.

If she was staying in the hotel, she'd have to go all the way down to the lobby to get to the other tower. However, if she got off on one of the floors between here and there, he was screwed. He'd have no way of knowing which one. As he'd threatened, he'd have to resort to bribing the concierge, though he doubted he'd have much luck.

By the time he made it to the first floor, his heart was thundering, though he wasn't sure if it was from running down the stairs, or from the excitement of chasing Sasha. At the door to the lobby, he paused to catch his breath and straighten his jacket. He swung open the door and stepped out, immediately scanning the lobby for her.

After a moment, one of the elevators chimed and opened. Sure enough, there was Sasha. From this distance, he could see her features no more clearly than he'd been able to up on the roof. He didn't dare get closer.

She seemed to hesitate, but then with a firm shake

of her head she spun around and headed straight for the hotel's courtesy phone. One phone call and fifteen minutes later, she was picked up outside the hotel. Not by a taxi. Not by a rental car. But by a man in a mud-splattered Jeep, with no top.

As he watched her through the plate-glass window of the hotel lobby he felt a surge of totally irrational jealousy. She'd said she didn't have a boyfriend.

Then the man chucked her on the chin, in an intimate—but decidedly not sexual—gesture. Not a boyfriend, then. And, presumably, not a husband or a fiancé. Her indignation on that subject, at least, had been genuine.

He could overlook the way she'd misled him on the other subjects. She wasn't staying at the hotel. Which meant there was a pretty good chance she worked in his building.

But if she did, why call a friend to pick her up? Why hadn't she driven herself home? And why was she so determined he not find out who she was?

She left him with many questions. All of which intrigued him even more. He would see her again on Friday. And if she didn't show up, it hardly mattered. Because if she did work in his building, it was only a matter of time before he found her again.

He hadn't recognized her.

As she stared out the open window of Keegan's Jeep that thought rattled around in her brain. Like the *clickity-clang* noise her car sometimes made, impossible to ignore and annoying as hell. A little frightening as well, like a portent of impending doom.

Tonight on the roof, when Reid had reached out to shake her hand—to introduce himself to her!—he might as well have kicked her in the teeth. It certainly wouldn't have hurt more.

Maybe she should have been prepared for it—after all, Pete hadn't recognized her, either. But it was one thing to have your geeky coworker not recognize you, and it was something else entirely to realize the man of your dreams—literally—couldn't pick you out of a lineup.

Unfortunately, Keegan wouldn't let her sit there, simmering in her own impotent angst.

"Tell me again why you needed me to pick you up."

She kept her attention on the passing buildings outside the window as he navigated through downtown. "I went up to the roof to eat dinner and ran into Reid."

"Babe, you're going to have to talk me through this one. Why did meeting your boss on the roof mean you couldn't drive yourself home?"

"He didn't recognize me."

"At first?"

"At all."

Keegan winced. "Ouch."

"And he hit on me."

"Oh." As Keegan turned south on Congress Avenue he was strangely silent. No witty comeback. No quip of bad advice.

Keegan's silence unsettled her. If he'd laughed off the experience or made a joke of it, she'd have had an easier time doing the same.

"He wanted to see me again," she added.

The silence seemed to hang between them. Keegan

waited until he'd crossed the river and was nearing her neighborhood before he asked, "What did you say?"

"I told him I'd meet him next Friday at the hotel." Then—for some reason she couldn't quite explain—she rushed to fill the strained silence with, "I'm not going to do it, though. That's why I had you pick me up. If I'd stopped at the office to pick up my car keys, he could have followed. He would have known who I am."

"So you're not going to meet him?"

"Absolutely not."

But even as she said the words, they didn't ring true. *Okay, Ms. Smarty-pants,* she said to herself, *if you're not going to meet him...if you were so hurt by him not recognizing you, then why did you ask him to stay? Why did you flirt with him? Why did you enjoy it so much?*

That certainly was the million-dollar question.

Yes, she'd been surprised that he hadn't recognized her. And, yes, she'd been a little hurt. But she'd also been intrigued.

She'd felt the strong tug she always felt around him, but for the first time she'd seen the spark of interest in his eyes. The lure of that mutual attraction was too strong to resist. Would she be strong enough to resist it next Friday?

Honestly, she couldn't say.

"You don't sound convinced," Keegan pointed out.

"I don't ever want him to know the woman he kissed tonight on the roof was Plain Jane Demeo."

"You kissed him?" Keegan's tone made it clear he thought she was insane. As if she needed confirmation.

"Yes...well, sort of. Actually, he kissed me." She just hadn't put up much of a fight.

"And you never told him who you are?"

"Good God, no." She laughed nervously. As Keegan slowed to a stop in front of her house, she shifted towards him. His face was cast in shadows, his expression unreadable. "Can you imagine someone like Reid actually going out on a date with me? I mean, if he knew who I was?"

Keegan stared straight ahead as he answered, "Yes, I can."

Then he turned towards her. She still couldn't read his expression, but he reached across the Jeep and chucked her on the chin. She took comfort in the familiarity of the action.

"Tell me what I should do."

"Can't do it. This one's up to you."

She stuck out her tongue at him in an expression of pure, childish disgust. "That's not fair. For ten years, you've been giving me bad, unwanted, and totally unwarranted advice. Now that I actually want your opinion about something, you change to a *laissez-faire* policy?"

"Okay, you really want my opinion?"

"Yes, please!"

"I think you should go for it. Get him out of your system. Have one night of great sex—or maybe just mediocre sex—and then you can go back to being yourself for the rest of your life. Unless you tell him who you are, he never has to know it's you. What have you got to lose?"

"My dignity. My job. My—"

"Don't worry about it. It's not like any of those things are really important to you, anyway, right?"

"That's really helpful. Thanks."

"Come on, I'm teasing. If he didn't recognize you

tonight, chances are good he won't recognize you next Friday."

"Okay, so he probably won't. But what if he does? Shouldn't I have a contingency plan or something? Just in case?"

Keegan, who'd never had a contingency plan in his life, looked annoyed. "Sure. If he recognizes you at work, you laugh it off. Lie and tell him you weren't really planning on meeting him."

"But—"

"Didn't you once say you didn't think Reid even knew who you were?"

She sighed. Keegan was right. She wouldn't need a contingency plan because Reid wasn't going to recognize her. He barely knew she existed. Which meant Keegan was right about something else, as well. If she was ever going to make her fantasies about Reid come true, it was now or never.

"You really think I should do this?"

Suddenly serious again, Keegan said, "If you don't, I think you'll regret it for the rest of your life."

And for a moment, she actually considered it. Next Friday night, she'd rent a hotel room, get all dolled up as Sasha, and seduce her boss. It was the stuff of fantasies.

Which was exactly the problem.

Sleeping with Reid was the stuff of fantasies. Her fantasies.

Unfortunately, the stuff of her fantasies was also the stuff of her work.

If she acted out her fantasies with Reid, what would happen to her creativity? To her mojo?

It would vanish, that was what.

Which meant, no matter how much she wanted to, there was no way Sasha could meet Reid next Friday night.

A week of "good ol' boy" networking with his father's buddy at *Trés Bien* had earned Forester+Blake a shot at the account. Reid had spent the whole time playing golf with the guy, eating barbecue he'd spent a fortune flying in from the Salt Lick in Austin, and singing the praises of his creative teams. He'd talked ad nauseam about innovative work Jane's group had done and espoused the benefits of hiring a smaller boutique company like Forester + Blake.

And, ironically, he hadn't been bored. Not even once. After a week of doing little but talk about Jane's work, he was more convinced than ever that only one thing would keep his fascination with Jane from turning into a full-blown obsession. A quick, mindless affair with Sasha.

It bothered him that he still didn't know her last name. That he knew next to nothing about her. Only that she worked in his building, liked hot and sweet peppers, and was the one woman on the planet who could make him forget about Jane.

Which meant he had to see Sasha again. Even if she didn't show up for their date tonight, he would find her. After all, he had her first name and a pretty good physical description—it had been dark, but not that dark. And, he had a partial license-plate number for her friend's Jeep. If it came down to it, he could find her through that.

Reid fingered the scrap of paper on which he'd scrawled 976-MR? as he waited for the elevator to take him up to the tenth floor. He glanced back down at the license plate number. How did you find someone from a license plate number? Nearly everything was available online these days, but he doubted that was. Did he know anyone in the police department who could help him out? Would he have to hire a private detective?

More importantly, had one evening with Sasha turned him into a psycho-stalker?

God, he hoped not.

The doors opened on the tenth floor and he nudged his way through the crowd and out into the hall. As he walked through the glass double doors with the words "Forester+Blake—Innovations in Advertising" written above them, he felt the weight of those words bear down on him.

He had a job to do—a business to run. Did he really need this kind of distraction?

As he passed the receptionist's desk he tapped his hand on the marble counter. "Morning, Polly."

"Hey, Reid. How'd the meeting go in New York?"

He paused, glancing back at the woman who'd been the receptionist here for as long as he could remember. Audrey had undoubtedly told Polly about the trip, but no one other than Matt knew whom he'd met with. So he smiled enigmatically. "Great."

Might as well give her something to gossip about.

Polly beamed. "That's good to hear. And you were meeting with…"

"Nice try."

Polly shrugged cheerfully and went back to her work on the computer.

He'd known her since he was fifteen and she was the prime example of why they desperately needed to win this *Trés Bien* account. A prime example of why he shouldn't let any woman—not Sasha and certainly not Jane—distract him from the work he needed to get done.

But at least an affair with Sasha wouldn't distract him at work. Much.

Trying to force his mind away from Sasha, he headed for the break room, only to stop in his tracks when he heard her voice. He stood there—his palm pressed to the swing door—listening.

There it was again...the self-conscious laughter followed by the sensual timbre of her voice. Definitely Sasha.

But what was she doing here? Was she some new employee he'd never met? Or maybe she worked on another floor, but had made friends with someone who worked for him.

Either way, he'd get to see Sasha even sooner than he'd hoped.

But when he swung open the door and walked into the break room, he saw only two people standing over by the coffee bar. Pete and a woman who had to be Sasha...but wasn't.

Jane Demeo hovered by the espresso machine, waiting for her latte, chatting with Pete. Chatting in Sasha's voice. She stood angled away from the door. She wore her hair tucked back into a ball cap and was dressed in jeans and a loose top that stretched the limits of Forester+Blake's lax dress code. If he hadn't heard her laugh, who knew when he would have put the pieces together?

Sasha was Jane Demeo.

CHAPTER SIX

"So you're definitely going through with it?" Keegan asked as soon as Jane answered her cell phone.

"Yes. For the gazillionth time, yes." She should have known better than to take a call from him at a time like this.

Tonight had to be perfect. This was, after all, her one. And only. Chance.

It was tonight or never. "Never" just didn't work for her.

As she pressed her cell phone to her ear she studied her reflection in the mirror of the hotel bathroom. Dorothea had come by earlier to do her hair and make-up. She'd brought with her a simple, low-cut black dress and a whole array of lingerie. Jane had been gartered, hosed, and pushed up. She had more infra-structure than the state highway department.

Once again, Plain Jane had been transformed into Sexy Sasha.

"What about your mojo?" Keegan asked.

She sighed. "With or without tonight, my mojo is gone."

"You know that's—"

"I know you don't believe me, but it's true. Seven days, Keegan. Seven whole days and I haven't had a single decent idea. Ever since he didn't recognize me on that rooftop, it's been a certified mojo drought."

Keegan laughed, making her fume with annoyance he couldn't see. "This isn't funny."

She studied her reflection in the mirror but found no signs of the frumpy, denim- and ball-cap-wearing woman she'd been just a few hours ago. No wonder Reid hadn't, either.

For an instant this morning, when he'd walked into the break room, she'd been sure he'd recognized her. His expression had clouded, his gaze had darkened. She'd been sure he was going to call her on it. But he hadn't. He hadn't said a word to her.

In retrospect, she could only assume he'd been annoyed to find an employee dressed so casually. Forester+Blake didn't have a dress code, *per se*. Sure, employees were expected to dress professionally when dealing with clients, but otherwise they could pretty much wear whatever they wanted. Still, today she'd been pushing it. Which only made her wonder if she subconsciously hadn't been trying to sabotage her plan.

She should be relieved. Shouldn't she?

Yes, of course she was. She didn't want him to recognize her. What she wanted was her mojo back.

"Look," she said into the phone as she turned away from the mirror. "This has to work. This is my only chance to get things back to normal. I need my mojo back. Especially since they've scheduled some big meeting for Monday. I think they're going to announce the coming layoffs. Which means I *have* to do this."

As she spoke, she moved through the hotel room; fluffing a throw pillow on the king-sized bed; turning the champagne, cooling in the bucket; setting the matches on the fireplace mantel.

"Look, darlin', I'm not saying you shouldn't do this. I just think you're crazy for thinking it's going to bring back your mojo."

"Well, it better," she snapped. "This hotel suite is costing me a fortune. If I get laid off now, I'll have to declare bankruptcy."

Financial bankruptcy was the least of her worries. It was the bankruptcy of ideas that scared her most.

He never intended to show up.

After realizing Jane and Sasha were the same woman, Reid had spent the entire day prowling around his office, trying to figure out exactly what Jane was up to. Half a dozen times, he'd stormed out of his office and made it nearly to her desk to demand an explanation, only to turn and storm back.

The Jane he knew would be petrified if her boss confronted her over this. But Sasha? Sasha would most likely just bump up her chin, meet him toe to toe and give as good as she got.

So which woman was she?

Jane, who harbored a crush on her boss, but was terrified of him? Or Sasha, who seemed ready to embark on a passionate affair with a stranger? He ached to find out.

What good would it do to meet her?

Yes, he could satisfy his curiosity, but nothing else.

She was an employee. Strictly, and by every definition, off limits.

So, he'd decided not to meet "Sasha" in the lobby at eight.

As long as he thought of her as Sasha, his resolution held. Bold and confident Sasha he could walk away from. But Jane? Shy, but brilliant, Jane was another matter altogether. As soon as he pictured Jane standing in the lobby—waiting for him to show up, finally leaving when he never did—he was lost.

Before he knew it, he was out the door and in the elevator, cursing every time it stopped between the tenth floor and the lobby, praying she hadn't already given up on him.

Finally, the elevator reached the first floor. He could barely wait while the people in front of him filed out through the doors.

He saw her as soon as he made it through the crowd. Even with most of the lobby separating them, he recognized her instantly.

Dressed in a low-cut black dress that clung to her tiny waist, then flared out over ample hips to swirl just about her knees, she looked like one of those pinup poster girls from the forties. Her hair fell in sculpted waves to her jawline. God, was she gorgeous. And from this distance, she was pure Sasha.

And yet, as he moved across the marbled lobby towards her, he saw hints of Jane in the tilt of her head, the slope of her shoulders, the lowered gaze. She stood and moved like a woman unaware of the power of her beauty. Unused to the sway she held over men.

How had he missed that on the roof?

Then she glanced in his direction, did a double take—proof she'd given up hope that he'd show—and, incrementally, she transformed completely into the woman she'd been a week ago. Shoulders back, lips curved into a pouty smile, head tilted so she gazed at him from under a veil of thick lashes.

He felt his gut tighten as she crossed the lobby. Why did he find her more attractive now that he knew she was Jane, now that he saw the vulnerability beneath the bravado?

And how the hell was he going to walk away from her?

Yet he would have to walk away. No matter what she had in mind, he couldn't sleep with her. Couldn't take advantage of her, not when he knew about the crush she had on him.

Maybe he could let her down easy. Take her out to dinner at a nice restaurant, then politely, and kindly, tell her it wasn't going to work out. Which she'd only believe if he managed to keep his hands off of her.

When she reached him, she tugged on his tie playfully. "You're late," she accused.

"I'm sorry." He found himself grasping for a lie. "I had a conference call with a client in New York that ran over."

Too late, he realized his mistake. Forester+Blake didn't have a client in New York. Yet.

Jane's eyes lit with curiosity. "A client in New York? But we don't—"

She broke off and it occurred to him that his slip might work to his advantage. Maybe he could get her to admit who she was if she was curious enough about the call.

He nodded towards the door. "You want to grab a bite to eat? I know this great Indian restaurant around the corner."

She shook her head. "No, I—"

"French, then? There's a place down on Sixth Street you'd like. Or maybe Cajun?" Anything to keep from following her back to her room. His self-control was suspect where she was concerned.

"We can order room service, if you're hungry."

She stepped closer, draping her hand on his arm, her fingers creeping up his sleeve.

Her voice sounded husky and sexy as hell. And he couldn't help wondering if she was trying to disguise it.

She didn't wait for his response, but sauntered over to the bank of hotel elevators and pushed the "up" arrow. Seconds later, a pair of doors opened and she stepped inside. With one palm pressed against the doors to keep them open, she asked, "You coming?"

Okay, he told himself. *Follow her up to her hotel room. Have a drink. You're just going to talk to her. To try to figure out what's going on. You'll be just fine.*

Whatever game she was playing, he had no intention of getting caught up in it. As long as he remembered that, he'd be fine. Right.

Before he could question his own intentions or willpower, he followed her into the elevator. The doors closed behind him, shutting out the rest of the world. She stood close to him, her shoulder touching his, and in the close space he was suddenly aware of her scent. He caught a whiff of the same perfume she'd worn last week, as well as the hint of apples.

Now that he knew Sasha was Jane, he recognized the scent. She always smelled like apples, he remembered. He just hadn't noticed it until now.

As the elevator lurched into motion, she said, "So tell me about this client of yours in New York."

She looked up at him as she spoke, and when he answered, he couldn't help gazing into her eyes.

"It's nothing." It'd be so easy to kiss her. He'd

only have to lower his head. She was so close. Mere inches away. And his body remembered all too well the feel of her in his arms. The taste of her mouth beneath his.

"Important enough that you kept me waiting," she reminded him.

Why had he kept her waiting? he wondered numbly for a second before sanity returned.

Even then, he ended up saying more than he meant to. "A potential client, actually. I was on the phone with the marketing director for *Trés Bien*. They—"

"The lingerie store?"

The surprise in her voice helped him knock off the lingering effects of her proximity. "Yeah, the lingerie store. They've put out a request for proposals."

"That's great!" Behind the Sasha façade he saw the glimmer of the real Jane in her excitement. "That would be a h-huge account."

"Yes, it would." Apparently she'd forgotten that he'd never mentioned where he worked, or even that he was in advertising. He didn't call her on it, though.

He watched with interest as she struggled to rein in her response. Watching her slip back and forth between the real Jane and the Sasha she pretended to be fascinated him.

"I mean, I'm sure that would be good for your business."

The elevator doors opened, and he followed her out into the hall. "We don't have the account yet. We've got a lot of hard work ahead of us."

He watched Jane carefully as he spoke. As soon as he'd mentioned *Trés Bien*, her eyes had lit up. He could practically see her mind working now.

When she spoke, her enthusiasm got the better of

her and she slipped back into her normal voice. "Oh, of course…but *Trés Bien*? How great would it be to w-work on that? I—" She blanched when she realized what she'd said. "I mean…you don't seem the type that minds hard work."

"I don't. What about you?"

She stopped outside the door to her room to pull the passkey from her bag. "What about me?"

"Do you mind hard work?"

She opened her mouth to respond, but stopped herself. He saw the glint of calculation in her gaze as she looked him up and down. "I don't mind hard anything."

He'd just bet she didn't.

Her voice—one hundred percent Sasha again—was full of sensual promise. He was almost annoyed with himself for responding to such a blatant come-on. Apparently it didn't take much from her to turn him on.

Then she opened the door to the hotel suite. Blindly, he followed her inside.

As he surveyed the room he felt his resistance slip another notch. The room was like something out of one of Jane's ads. The Butler Steam Vac ad, to be precise.

The curtains had been pulled back to reveal the glittering Austin skyline. A fireplace dominated one wall, the king-sized bed the other. Both were ready for use. And he couldn't help wondering which would be hotter, the fire or the sex. Too bad he'd never know.

To the left of the fireplace, champagne was chilling in a silver bucket. A pair of champagne flutes sat on the fireplace mantel. Just as in her drawings.

Well, at least he had the answer to one of his questions about Jane. He'd wondered earlier what the hell kind of game she was playing. Now he knew. She wasn't playing a game. She was acting out a fantasy.

He wanted to be offended. He wished he could have been annoyed. But the truth was, the scene before him was more tempting than he wanted to admit.

Worse still, he knew how she wanted this to play out. How he wanted it to play out, for that matter. Over and over, the scene unspooled in his mind.

The setting was charming, but not necessary. The fireplace, the romantic music, and champagne were all just props, background noise. Nonsense, really. As soon as he pulled her into his arms they'd fade from his awareness. When he felt her body against his, nothing else would matter. Nothing but the heat of her mouth against his, the desperation of her hands as they stroked his skin, and the fervor of her response to him.

He'd tried to banish the fantasy from his mind. God, how he'd tried. But it hadn't worked.

Meeting her as "Sasha" the other night had only made things worse. He could no longer pretend the body she hid beneath her baggy clothes was not worth seeing. He no longer had to imagine how her lips would feel beneath his. But it wasn't Sasha he wanted. It was Jane.

As he watched her cross to the fireplace, one thought echoed in his mind: Man, he'd screwed up. He should not have come here.

She bent over to light the fire, the fabric of her dress stretched taut against the curve of her buttocks. No anemic, hard lines to her body. No, Jane was all lush curves and generous flesh.

She straightened and met his gaze. The gleam of anticipation in her eyes was far more potent than even her curves.

"Would you like a glass of champagne?"

"Sure." A glass of champagne? An icy shower? A sexual harassment lawsuit? Whatever. "Actually, no. I, um…I shouldn't have come."

She frowned. Not the exaggerated pout she'd put on before, but a genuine frown. "You're not leaving?"

"I think I better." He backed up a step.

"But you just got here." She followed, steadily closing the distance between them. "Surely you can stay for just one drink."

Now, she was standing close enough for him to touch her, to trace his finger along the arch of her cheek or the slope of her neck, to lean forward and kiss her.

He jammed his hands into his pockets and rocked back on his heels. "If I stayed, you don't really think it would be for just one drink, do you?"

She shook her head and her hair brushed against her cheek in exactly the spot he wanted to brush his lips. "No."

"Then I think I better go."

He turned to leave, but she stopped him with a hand on his arm. "Why?"

Her touch seemed to burn through the fabric of his jacket and shirt. He searched her gaze for any sign that she might come clean with him, but knew she was far past the point of honest confession.

Unsure what else to tell her, he said, "This—" he nodded to indicate the hotel room "—isn't the kind of thing I normally do."

She jerked her hand away from his arm, her expression horrified. "You think it's the kind of thing *I* normally do?"

"I don't know." But he suspected not.

Still, he saw the hurt in her eyes. The hint of vulner-ability that pulled at him so.

His instincts roared at him to touch her, and before he could stop himself, his fingers grazed her cheek. "This just wouldn't be wise," he murmured.

"I've been wise my whole life, Reid. I'm ready to be reckless."

She met his gaze boldly as she spoke, and he realized for the first time that her eyes weren't merely brown. They were hazel, with pale green rimming her dilated pupils.

In that instant, something pushed him over the edge. Maybe it was the way she said his name, without her normal hesitation or stuttering shyness. Or maybe it was the startling realization that, after five years, he hadn't even known what color her eyes were. Or maybe it was the way her words spoke to him.

He felt her pull deep in his soul. Desire snaked through him, but this was more than just a physical reaction to a beautiful woman. She seemed to have looked inside him. To know him better than he knew himself.

When she leaned forward, rising up onto her toes to kiss him, he didn't pull away. She was right. He'd been wise for far too long. The recklessness he struggled to keep buried deep inside of him broke free.

In that instant all his careful plans to remain aloof—to resist Jane—vanished.

As soon as he felt her lips pressed to his, he wrapped his hands around her bare arms and pulled her to him. He barely registered her gasp of surprise, but the low moan that tore through her told him all he needed to know.

Her mouth was unbelievably hot beneath his. He re-membered how she'd tasted the last time. Hot and sweet, like the peppers. This time, she tasted sweet and crisp—like champagne—and he couldn't help wondering if she'd sampled some to build up her courage.

Aching to feel her generous curves against him, he found himself pulling her even closer. He felt the weight of her breasts brush his chest, felt the gentle slope of her tummy against his hardening penis. Felt her hands tugging at his clothes, shoving his jacket off his shoulders.

He released her only long enough to shake his jacket free, and pulled her back to him before it even hit the floor. He wrapped one arm across her back, grabbing her buttocks to raise her up to him.

One of her hands clung to his shoulder. She buried the other in his hair, urging his head across her mouth. Following her lead, he tore his mouth from hers to trail kisses down the length of her neck.

"This is insane," he gasped between kisses.

"No." She raised one of her legs up to his hip, deepening the contact between them. "This is perfect. Just perfect."

She gasped as she rubbed the apex of her thighs against his erection. The blood pounding through him quickened as he felt a shudder course through his body.

His fingers itched to pull her dress from her body, to unwrap her like a present, to lose himself in the exploration of her body. An even deeper need pulsed through him. The need to possess her completely. To bury himself inside her and feel her shudder with pleasure.

The image from her drawing flashed through his mind: The picture of a man cradled between a woman's thighs, her hips bucked up towards him. His erection surged at the thought of laying Jane on the floor and feeling her legs wrapped around him.

Instinctively, he backed her up, step by step, towards

the swath of carpet in front of the fireplace. He didn't lift his mouth from her body. With each step, her moans of passion heightened his own arousal.

A shudder coursed through her and she arched towards him. "Yes," she panted. "Oh, please, yes."

The passion lacing her words nearly drove him over the edge. He'd never make it to the fireplace. He had to have her now.

Grabbing the hem of her dress, he lifted it up and over her head in one fast motion. Though he ached to explore her body slowly, that would have to wait. He'd need hours, maybe days, to learn all her secrets. He had neither the patience nor the self-control to wait. For now, the feel of her velvety skin would have to be enough.

As he lowered her to the floor, she sought the closure of his pants. As her fingers brushed against his erection, he squeezed his eyes closed and bit back a groan.

When he felt her thighs clench his hips, he could only mutter, "Oh, Jane, you're killing me."

He lowered his mouth back to hers, but found her lips stiff and unyielding beneath his. He pulled back to see her expression. She gaped at him, wide-eyed.

It took his lust-addled brain several beats to catch up. "Jane, what's wrong?"

Her hands shoved at his chest. Instinctively, he braced his palms beside her shoulders, giving her enough room to crab walk back from him.

"What did you just call me?"

CHAPTER SEVEN

SHOCK AND CONFUSION reeled through Jane. "What did you call me?" she repeated.

Reid's expression was clouded with passion. Clearly dazed, he rocked back onto his heels. "Jane. I called you Jane."

Hearing her name on his lips was like a splash of cold water. Unfortunately, the water hit only her mind, not her body. Her body still trembled with awareness and ached for completion.

She staggered to her feet. "You knew?"

Scrubbing a hand down his face, he said, "I realized today. This morning in the break room."

"And you didn't say anything?" Her words came out like an accusation.

Instead of answering, he studied her as he stood. Though several feet separated them, she felt his gaze like a caress. She wore only her bra, panties, garter, and stockings.

She suddenly felt intensely aware of her near-naked state. She'd always thought her body was far from perfect. Too round. Too soft. But the appreciative gleam in Reid's gaze made her feel lush and desirable.

Without the warmth of his body over hers, the cool air in the room chilled her skin, hardening her nipples even more. Suddenly self-conscious, she longed for something to cover her body with.

Before she could even reach for her dress, he spoke. "Unless you want to pick up where we left off, I suggest you put your dress back on."

"I was just about to." She pointed to his feet. "You're standing on it."

He handed her the dress, watching her as she turned it inside out and slipped it over her head. When she'd finally tugged the dress into place, he turned his attention to the champagne and the glasses.

"You're pouring yourself a glass of champagne?" Her voice rose with indignation.

"I think we could both use a drink. Unless you've got a bottle of Scotch hidden away somewhere, this will have to do."

He poured two glasses and handed her one. She held the glass in both hands to keep her trembling fingers from spilling it. The unsated desire still churning her blood turned to agitation.

Maybe he was right. Maybe a drink would calm her nerves, but she couldn't bring herself to raise the glass to her lips. After all the times she'd dreamt of sipping champagne with him, it seemed a travesty to drink this now.

He had no such compunction. Then again, he hadn't been fantasizing about tonight for five years.

She crossed to the pair of chairs by the window and lowered herself into one of them. She set the glass on the side table and rested her head in her hands.

"I can't believe you knew who I was and you still

came." She murmured the words, more to herself than to him.

"I can't believe you honestly thought I wouldn't figure it out." He followed her across the room and sat in the other chair.

Her gaze snapped up to his. "It was a logical assumption," she defended. "You didn't recognize me that night on the roof."

"It was dark. And you looked different."

She couldn't argue with that, so she didn't bother trying. "Why did you come here tonight?"

He took another drink, then answered without meeting her gaze. "Curiosity, I guess."

God, this was worse than she'd thought.

Suddenly glad she had something to do with her hands, she raised the glass and drank deeply. Then she nearly choked when he said, "I know about the drawings."

She set the glass aside carefully. "What drawings?"

"The Butler Steam Vac pitch. I know that's me in the drawings."

"It's n—"

"It's my ring." He held up his right hand, twisting it to show off the ring, and then the side. "It's my scar."

"I…" Her heart pounded as she realized the impact of his words. Her breath came in short, fast bursts and her mind raced. As if she had no control over herself, words burst forth. "Oh, God. This is bad." She stood and began to pace. "I can't believe I did that. I can't believe you noticed." *Oh, how embarrassing.*

She glanced in his direction and noticed he was smiling as he watched her. "This isn't funny," she snapped. "If you figured it out, other people could, too."

He stood. "If it makes you feel any better, I'm sure no one else would notice. The scar is barely visible."

She hardly registered his words. "And then," she rushed on, "I invite you up here to seduce you. And then, you came? Oh, this is so bad."

"Calm down," he murmured reassuringly. "It's not that bad."

"Not that bad? I could get fired over this."

"Fired?" he asked with a laugh. "I'm not going to fire you."

She glared at him. "This isn't funny."

"Actually, it kind of is."

"Yeah, well, your job isn't at stake."

When she turned back around, she found him standing beside her. He rubbed his hand up her arm in an action he must have meant to be calming. "I promise I'm not going to fire you."

His hand felt warm and strong against her skin. His touch sent shivers of pleasure through her body. Far from reassuring, it only reminded her of how close they'd come to having sex.

And now she would never get to sleep with him. She was suffering all the negative repercussions of sleeping with her boss, without getting to experience any of the mind-blowing pleasure. This sucked.

She shifted her gaze from where his hand rested on her arm up to his eyes. This close, his eyes were an even more vivid green than they normally seemed. As she studied his face, she realized that—despite his relaxed demeanor—he was still aroused. She could see it in his eyes and in the strain of his smile.

His hand slowed to a sensuous caress that she felt

all the way to the tips of her toes. She felt herself swaying towards him, when he jerked his hand from her arm and put some distance between them.

As he crossed back to his champagne glass, he said, "Stop blaming yourself for this. It's my fault." He took a long drink, then added, "And stop worrying about your job. Whatever would have happened between us, it would have been safe. I need you too much to let you go."

Something deep within her responded to his words. Something she didn't want to analyze.

Turning away from his scrutiny, she wrapped her arms around her waist and went to stand by the fireplace. "Thank you. That's very kind."

"I didn't say it to be kind. I said it because it's true." His voice was edged with just a hint of exasperation.

She turned back to study him, but the lighting in the room was too dim for her to read his expression.

"I've annoyed you," she said.

"No."

"Yes, I have. I can hear it in your voice."

"Okay," he admitted. "I like it better when you're being honest with me."

"Honest? I've tried to pass myself off as another person. This isn't me at my most honest."

"Bad word choice. Not honest, exactly. More open, I guess. Less timid. When you're not trying so hard to be the perfect employee."

"I see." So he liked her better as Sasha than as Jane. That wasn't surprising.

So why did it hurt?

"Look, Jane, you're an important part of the company. Your team does some of our best work."

"Well, Teresa—"

"Teresa is a good team leader. She's a great presenter, but we both know you're the creative mind behind your team's work."

"We do? I mean—" she swallowed, trying not to sound too hopeful "—you know that?"

He came to stand beside her by the fireplace. "What kind of CEO do you think I'd be if I didn't know that?"

"I'm sorry," she said. She wished he weren't standing so close, but he made it hard for her to concentrate on his words. "I didn't mean to insult you."

"You're doing it again."

"What?"

"Being timid."

"Well, I'm sorry." This time her words were sarcastic rather than apologetic. "I'm not used to talking back to the CEO."

He smiled. "That's better." He brushed his knuckle down her cheek. "Don't forget, I may be the CEO, but the job you do is much more important than mine. This company wouldn't work without you. The most important thing I do is make sure the creatives are happy."

"And that's more important than…oh, say, running the company?"

"Without people like you, there's no company to run."

"I've never thought of it that way."

He shoved his hands into his pockets. "Tonight was a mistake. We both know that. But I don't want it to make you feel nervous or uncomfortable. I don't want it to affect your work."

"It won't." She wished, though, that she felt even half as sure of that as she sounded.

"Good. The whole company will be working on the presentation for *Trés Bien*."

"The whole company?"

"Yes. It's important enough that I want everyone's input. But, to be honest, I think you're our best bet. We need something fun and fresh. Something sexy."

His eyes dropped to her lips, and she knew he was remembering what it had been like to kiss her.

Clearing his throat, he tore his gaze from her face to stare into the fireplace. "Fresh, fun, and sexy is what you do best."

"Okay, then. The whole company is depending on me to come up with something fresh, fun, and sexy. Great. I'll get right on that."

His chuckle told her he appreciated her sarcasm. "No pressure, though, okay? I only told you so you'd stop worrying about losing your job."

Somehow, that didn't help. Yes, she felt better knowing her job was safe for now. But what if they didn't get the *Trés Bien* account? More to the point, what if they didn't get the account because she couldn't come up with a halfway decent idea?

What then?

Unfortunately, she had all weekend to worry about it.

Walking out of Jane's hotel room had been one of the hardest things he'd ever done. It took him most of the weekend to convince himself he'd made the right choice. The only choice.

Jane was too important to Forester+Blake for him to risk getting involved with her. Which shouldn't have been a problem. Work always came first in his life. That was the way it was. When his father had died while he'd still been in graduate school, he'd promised himself he'd do right by the company. He'd always known his father had dreams of them working side by side.

But Reid had never really wanted to work in the ad business, so he'd taken his time in college. And then in graduate school. He'd studied abroad and been in and out of several independent study programs, telling himself and his father that he just wanted a really solid liberal arts education before he finally settled into the MBA program at Stanford. Then, just before Reid had finally finished school, his father had died of a heart attack.

Reid had dropped everything and finally come home. Sure, he ran Forester+Blake mostly out of guilt, but what else could he do? If he'd come home earlier, his father might still be alive. At the very least, they could have worked together for a few years.

The company had to come first. He owed it to his father.

He was still telling himself that Monday when Matt stopped by his office.

"Everything all set for the meeting this afternoon?" Matt asked from the doorway.

"It's getting there." Reid looked up from the paperwork he wasn't reading. "Why do you ask?"

"You were here pretty late on Friday night." Matt propped his shoulder against the door and crossed his arms over his chest. "Plus, the security log showed you'd stopped by over the weekend. I thought you might have been finishing up something for the meeting."

"Just paperwork," he lied. In reality, he'd come to the office on Saturday to look up Jane's address. The first time, he'd talked himself out of it and gone home before his computer was even booted up. But then, he'd come back on Sunday. He'd driven by her house that evening. He'd even parked his car a couple of houses down while he'd talked himself out of going in.

It shouldn't have been as hard as it had been to slide

his car into gear and drive away. This business was his life. He'd given up more important things for it before. So why couldn't he get Jane out of his head?

Luckily Matt didn't see through his lie. He just nodded and then asked, "You've already decided on a team to head this up, right?"

"Yep." Reid nodded, mentally bracing himself for the argument he knew would come. "Teresa's team."

After a second of consideration, Matt frowned. "Isn't Teresa on leave?"

"She'll be gone until the fifteenth." He held up his hand to ward off Matt's protests. "I know, by the time she gets back, all the work will be done. If we're lucky, she can step in right at the end to do the presentation. If we're not lucky, she won't make it in time. Worst-case scenario, you or I will end up doing the pitch."

With his hands propped low on his hips, Matt just shook his head. "Teresa's team? Without Teresa? That's—"

"They're still the best we've got. Even without her."

"Man, I don't know. It's a huge risk."

Reid stood and rounded his desk. He propped his hips on the edge and stretched his feet out in front of him. "Trust me. Jane is ready for this. I can feel it."

Matt pinned Reid with an assessing stare. "You sure about this?"

"Yeah." And with that, Reid straightened, effectively ending the conversation, and crossed his office. "You want to grab some lunch?"

"Sure."

Reid grabbed his jacket from the coatrack by the door and pushed his arms through the sleeves as he shut the door behind him.

"You seeing someone new?" Matt asked as they made their way down the hall.

Reid stumbled, but hoped that Matt hadn't noticed. "No. Why?"

"Your jacket smells like perfume." Matt patted him on the shoulder.

"It does?" Reid raised his arm to his face and sniffed. Sure enough, the spicy scent of Jane's perfume wafted up to him.

"Yep."

"I went shopping over the weekend," he quickly lied. "Made the mistake of walking past the cosmetics counter in the department store."

"That's the worst lie I've ever heard." Matt shook his head. "You're slipping. When you were a kid, you could lie through your teeth."

"That's not something I'm proud of," Reid pointed out.

"Besides, whenever you're seeing someone, you feel guilty. Like you're abandoning the company or something. You always end up putting in more hours. Coming in on weekends, that kind of thing."

Reid felt a twinge of guilt. In the past, that may have been true, but this time around it wasn't.

As they reached the elevators, he turned to Matt. "Does Forester+Blake have a policy about intra-office dating?"

Matt seemed to consider for a minute. "Not that I know of." Matt pressed the down button. "Why? Does your new girlfriend work here?"

Reid didn't like the speculative gleam in Matt's eyes. "I don't have a new girlfriend."

Matt chuckled. "Well, if your mystery woman changes status, let me know."

"There is no mystery woman."

Not anymore. Now that he knew who Sasha was, wasn't he supposed to lose interest? Wasn't that the plan?

Or had the plan been that Sasha was supposed to make him lose interest in Jane?

Either way, finding out that Sasha and Jane were one and the same had really screwed up his plan. And if he wasn't careful, this debacle would screw up more than just his plan. It'd screw up his life.

CHAPTER EIGHT

"You're late," Pete whispered as Jane slid onto the chair beside him.

"Oh, really? I h-hadn't noticed." Then, to soften the sarcasm, she added, "Thanks for saving me a spot."

Thank God Pete had picked seats towards the back of the room. For company meetings, Forester+Blake always rented a conference room at the Prescott Hotel large enough to accommodate their eighty-odd employees. Usually these meetings were an annual event. Since the formal company meeting had taken place less than four months ago, she could only assume Reid was planning some big announcement about *Trés Bien*.

But for now, Matt Blake was up on stage giving a warm-up speech about the "innovative creative style" Forester+Blake was known for. Rousing though it was, she couldn't be sorry she'd missed most of it. In fact, she'd nearly missed work altogether.

After Friday night, she wasn't sure she was up to facing Reid dressed as herself. And yet, there was no point in continuing the charade. He knew Sasha was a fraud. The easiest way to put this whole nightmare behind her was to bury Sasha forever.

The thought made her a little sad. She'd almost miss—

"Did you hear that?" Pete elbowed her sharply.

Her gaze jerked to Pete's face. "Huh?"

"Stop daydreaming," he said in a whispered hiss. "This is important."

"What?" she grumbled. But when she looked up, she realized Reid had taken the stage.

"It's about *Trés Bi—*"

"Shh."

Pete shot her an annoyed look, but quieted, turning his attention to Reid, just as she had. As always, she promised herself she'd actually listen to what he had to say. But as always, she found herself studying him instead, fascinated by the heavy lock of dark brown hair that fell across his forehead, by the sharp motion of his hand gestures and the way he always kept one hand tucked firmly in his pants pocket.

He wore a Bugs Bunny tie today and she wondered if he was feeling clever and confident or if she merely read too much into his choice of ties. As he spoke, he kept rocking up onto the balls of his feet, as if he wanted to pace, but wouldn't allow himself.

He'd paced her hotel room the other night. Of course, the other night he'd done a lot of things he didn't normally do. Since she was better off not thinking about that night, she tried again to focus on his words.

"...which is why we're up to the challenge," he was saying.

Around the room, she noticed her coworkers nodding in agreement, whispering to each other in their excitement.

"With a project this big, we'll need everyone on board and fully committed. Everyone in the company will need to pitch in. Even if you're not working on the project yourself, you'll be working with others who are. And we'll need the help picking up the slack on other projects."

He seemed to be looking at her as he spoke. Was this his way of telling her she wouldn't be working on the ad? If so, that would mean his whole "you're the most important member of my team" crap was...well, total crap.

She stood, ready to sneak out the back door, when she heard him say, "That's why Jane and Pete will be the lead team on this project."

As she straightened she felt every eye in the room turn in her direction.

As Jane waited for the rest of Forester+Blake to leave the conference room, she tried not to listen to the nervous chatter. However, it was impossible to block it all out. As she stood off to the side, waiting to talk to Reid and get this whole thing straightened out, she caught the occasional snippet of conversation.

"Jane Demeo? Can you believe it?"

"What is he thinking?"

"Never heard of her. Are you sure she works here?"

And—her personal favorite—"Jane Demeo is a moron. I don't know about the rest of you, but I'm sending out my résumé now."

She gritted her teeth, trying to force her lips into some semblance of a smile. Then she heard the moron comment. Why bother? It'd be so much easier to just poison the idiot's coffee. Not to mention more enjoyable.

Damn it, she was tired of people treating her as if she were slow—a moron—simply because she stuttered. Now, more than ever, she wished she'd dressed as Sasha today. Instead she'd worn a simple denim dress, as nondescript as she was, with her short, high-lighted hair pulled back with a clip and her face devoid of makeup. She really could have used Sasha's confidence right now.

"You don't look happy."

She turned to find Reid standing behind her. The auditorium had emptied, leaving them essentially alone. "Should I?"

Reid studied her for a moment. "Most people would be. This is a big opportunity for you."

He started walking towards the door and she had to follow. "An opportunity? An opportunity to fail in front of the wh-wh-whole company. That's wh-what it is."

Damn it, she hadn't wanted to stutter. It would be really nice if just once Reid could see her as a calm and collected professional. Not as a nervous, stuttering mess. Not as a sexual piranha bent on seducing him. Just as a competent employee.

Reid merely smiled, looking not at all worried. "You won't fail."

When they reached the doors to the auditorium, she braced her hand on the door, keeping it closed, "N-n-no-o-one here believes I can do this job."

"I do."

The simplicity of his statement, the conviction in his eyes, rattled her. Hell, his mere closeness rattled her. She did her best to shake it off.

"I'm not qualified to lead a project like this."

"You weren't paying attention."

"Huh?"

Reid shook his head as if scolding her, but the smile

tugging at his lips told her he was teasing. "First you show up late and then you don't even pay attention?"

Her heart thudded in her chest with a teenager's fear of getting caught skipping class or breaking curfew. Fear, yes, but excitement as well.

"I was paying—" she began to protest before he cut her off.

"If you'd been listening, you'd know that I don't intend for you to run the project."

"Y-you don't?" She looked back at the stage, mentally replaying what she remembered from his speech.

But she had been sitting there like a dope, fantasizing about Reid, so maybe she'd misheard him. Great.

"I was distracted." She felt her cheeks warm. "If y-you didn't say Pete and I are leading the project, then wh-wh-what did you say?"

His lips curled into a slow, sexy smile. The kind of smile that made her belly clench and her imagination work overtime. "I said I'd be heading up the project and you would be working directly under me."

"Oh."

Oh, my.

Working directly under Reid Forester? Off the top of her head, she could think of dozens—no, hundreds— of things she'd love to do directly under Reid. Working was pretty far down on the list.

Her cheeks burned even hotter. And, at the moment, her cheeks weren't even her hottest body part. Her body seemed so tuned in to his. And nearly sleeping with him on Friday night only made things that much worse. Now that she knew what it felt like to be almost naked and writhing beneath him, how could she stand here and not think about it?

"But—" she struggled to come up with something semi-intelligent and not at all sexual to say "—you never head up projects."

He arched his eyebrow playfully. "You think I'm not up to the job?"

Which was worse? Coming on to your boss or insulting his abilities? "I didn't mean that. I was just making an observation."

"I think I can handle it." Wrapping his fingers around her wrist, he gently removed her hand from the door, then opened it.

Her skin tingled where he'd touched her and she had to fight the impulse to rub off the effects of his touch. She walked briskly to keep up with him as he worked his way to the elevators. "The thing is, Mr. Forester, I'm not sure—"

He stopped abruptly, and she nearly ran into him. "Don't you think you should call me Reid? Under the circumstances, Mr. Forester-ing me is a little absurd."

"I thought w-we agreed to forget what happened Friday night," she said through clenched teeth.

"I was referring to the circumstances of us working closely together." He smiled suggestively. "But it's nice to know you haven't forgotten it, either."

Either?

Oh, my, indeed.

Before she could get her thundering pulse under control, he started walking again. "I know what you're going to say, Jane."

"Y-y-you do?"

"You're going to throw out the same protests you did the other night. You don't have enough experience. There are better people for the job. Et cetera, et cetera."

In fact, that had been what she'd been about to say. She didn't like that he found her so predictable.

"Those arguments are just as true now as they were then," she pointed out.

"Those arguments are all in your head."

"What are you saying? That I'm delusional?"

He laughed. They reached the elevators and he pushed the button. "I wouldn't go that far. Let's just say, you tend to downplay your abilities."

She stiffened, crossing her arms over her chest. "I resent that."

In a decidedly non-bosslike gesture, he reached out to grasp her chin. He nudged her jaw until she met his gaze. "And I resent that you don't trust me. I know what I'm doing."

She pulled in a deep breath and was hit with the scent of his cologne. But it was the husky intimacy of his tone that sent shivers down her spine and the gentle persistence of his touch that made her ache to close the distance between them.

The doors to the elevator opened with a *ding* and he dropped his hand. "Come on, Jane, be honest." He stepped into the otherwise empty elevator and she followed. As the doors closed behind her, he said, "Just between the two of us, admit it. You know you're good."

His voice dropped even lower as he spoke. Suddenly the elevator seemed incredibly tiny. Unbelievably close and intimate.

She felt his words like a caress as he coaxed the response he wanted. "Just admit it. You. Are. Good."

"I am good," she confessed. The expression in his eyes darkened and she suddenly wished she were talking about her abilities in bed rather than her ability to write copy. "I'm very good."

But she didn't feel good. She felt very, very bad. Downright naughty, in fact. For an instant, the line between Jane and Sasha blurred.

He leaned in even closer and she imagined she heard him suck in a deep breath. She tilted her chin up, begging him with her eyes to kiss her again.

Had it been mere days since he'd last kissed her? It felt like weeks—years even—since she'd felt his body pressed against hers. Felt his heart pounding beneath her touch. Felt his hands stroking her flesh.

The elevator jerked to a stop and the doors swooshed open. She jerked away from him, putting enough distance between each other to fool anyone watching into thinking they were talking about just business.

Which we were, she reminded herself.

Reid merely smiled, looking smug and confident. And so damn sexy it was all she could do not to push the "close the doors" button, trap him in the elevator and have her way with him right there against the elevator wall. Who cared if the entire office knew what they were doing? Not her, apparently.

This thing with Reid was seriously getting out of control.

Trying to get ahold of her rampaging hormones and hoping to avoid being the object of office-wide speculation, she whispered, "I'll give it some thought, okay?"

Before she could beat a hasty retreat, Reid caught up with her and wrapped his hand around her arm. "Oh, no, you don't," he whispered back, steering her towards his office.

"People are staring," she hissed under her breath.

"No, they're not." But as they passed his assistant's desk, Audrey stared openly. He laughed. "Maybe a little. Get used to it."

She dug in her heels and pulled her arm free. "Wh-what's that supposed to mean?"

He ignored her and turned to Audrey. "Can you bring us a couple cups of coffee? Decaf cappuccino for me. Latte, two sugars, extra foam for Jane." He shot her an assessing look. "Right?"

Audrey nodded and, without waiting for Jane's reply, bustled off to fetch the coffee.

"How do you know how I like my coffee?" she asked.

"I'm observant." With a hand pressed to her lower back, he guided her towards his office.

"Nobody's that observant."

The corner of his mouth twitched in a wry smile. "You were making coffee the other day when I realized you were Sasha."

She blinked in surprise. "So?"

"Let's just say there are several things about that moment that are burned into my memory."

"Oh."

As the door clicked shut behind them she was suddenly aware of how alone they were. This was much worse than being alone with him in the elevator. This was private. No elevator doors to whoosh open at any inopportune moment.

Yes, the rest of the company was right outside, and, yes, Audrey would return soon with their coffee. But no one would enter Reid's office without his permission. For all intents and purposes, they were as alone right now as they had been last Friday night in the hotel room.

His hand still rested at her back, warm and strong, through the thin fabric of her dress. What would he do—she couldn't help wondering—if she closed the distance between them? If she kissed him?

Loosen his tie, shuck off his jacket, and they could almost pick up right where they'd left off. Sure, there was no fire, no champagne, and no king-sized bed. But there was something almost better.

His desk. His executive leather chair. How many times had she imagined making love to him there?

An image flashed through her mind of him sitting in that chair, naked except for a pair of silk boxer shorts. She sat across from him, perched on the edge of his desk. Black lace teddy, garters, sheer stockings, black three-inch heels… No. Make that black leather riding boots. The toe of one of those boots propped on the edge of the chair, just between Reid's parted legs, just inches from his—

"God, Jane, I would love to know what you're thinking right now."

Reid's huskily muttered words brought the real world sharply back into focus.

"What?" she asked dumbly, her body throbbing, every instinct she had screaming at her to mold herself to him.

He brushed a lock of her hair from her face and tucked it behind her ear. "It's not the first time I've seen you do that."

"What?" Her voice sounded breathless, which was not surprising since her heart was beating faster than it did after one of her power yoga classes.

"You do it in meetings all the time. Your eyes dilate and get kind of spacey. It's like you're in your own little world."

Her own little world? Her own little fantasy world.

Her cheeks burned with embarrassment and she forced herself to take a step back. "I don't know wh-what y-you're talking about."

"Sure you do. You—" A knock on the door interrupted him.

He closed his eyes, ducking his head slightly as he exhaled. Was that regret flicking across his expression?

A second later, whatever she thought she saw vanished as he raised his head and called out, "Come on in, Audrey."

She was grateful for Audrey's interruption and used the reprise to lower herself to one of the brown leather chairs opposite Reid's desk.

Audrey handed her the coffee cup. As Audrey left, Reid settled across from her, resting on the edge of his desk, legs stretched out in front of him as he eyed her over the edge of his cup.

"I know I shouldn't ask—hell, I probably don't want to know—but when you do that 'your own little world' thing you're just… I don't know, estimating your taxes or something, right? I mean, you're not thinking about anything…in particular."

It had to be the first time she'd ever seen him flustered. It was hard to believe, but he had to be even sexier like this. Or maybe it was just the idea that he was flustered because of her that was so sexy.

But whatever it was, it wasn't helping matters.

So she took a fortifying sip of coffee, then said, "No, n-nothing in particular. Estimating my taxes. Calculating the national debt. Trying to remember the digits of Pi, that kind of thing."

"Nothing interesting at all, then?"

If possible, she felt her cheeks burn even hotter. "Nope. Not at all."

But the expression in his eyes told her he knew she was lying. "That's good," he said with a sigh. "Because if you were thinking of something…at all interesting, that would only make this situation harder."

"Yes, much harder," she agreed, wishing fervently that things were getting harder by the minute.

For a long moment, he just watched her. She felt his gaze deep within her, like a physical caress. Like the familiar touch of a lover.

Then, abruptly, he straightened, moved away from his desk and from her. "I know you're worried about this project, Jane, but you don't need to be."

He'd changed topics so quickly, it took her a second to catch up. She thought about what he'd said earlier about her not trusting him. She didn't want him to think that, especially since—whether he'd ever admit it or not—his new role must be as scary for him as hers was for her.

She didn't want him to think she doubted his abilities. At the same time, she really wanted him to take her seriously. So she sucked in a deep breath, thrust back her shoulders and summoned all the Sasha she could muster. "It's not that I don't think I can do the job. Others don't think I can."

"Does that really matter?"

"To you? Maybe not." Probably not. Reid was always the picture of self-confidence. He probably didn't understand these kinds of fears. "But it matters to me. And whether you want to admit it or not, it matters to the company."

"I don't see—"

"In times like these, people need a strong leader. And they need to know they can trust their leader."

"This sounds like something out of one of Roosevelt's fireside chats."

"'The only thing we have to fear is fear itself'? That's not far from the truth. All I'm saying is, no one in this company will be doing their best work if they think you've made a bad decision."

"No problem, then. All we have to do is convince people you're up to the job."

"As if it were that easy."

"It is that easy."

"What? Exude self-confidence while single-handedly saving the company?"

"Don't forget, I'll be right there with you."

As if that helped matters. With him right beside her she was twice as likely to make a total ass of herself.

He must have seen the doubts in her eyes, because he added, "I've seen you do it." His voice dropped a notch. "That night we met up on the roof, you were self-confident and sexy as hell. You knocked my socks off. You did it to the guys from Butler, too."

"That's different."

"How?"

"The guys from Butler didn't know me. They had no expectations. No preconceptions."

"You can't let other people's preconceptions about you run your life. This is your job we're talking about. This is your future and the future of the company. What's more important? Holding on to your fears or winning this account?"

Faced with a question like that, she couldn't even meet his gaze anymore. He'd stated it so simply, in such obvious terms, that her arguments against working on the project suddenly seemed selfish and childish.

As if sensing he was about to win her over, he pushed just a little harder. "Come on, Jane, I know you can do this. I need you to do this."

How could she resist that? How could she sit there, listen to Reid all but beg her, and still protest at all?

She stood, forcing herself to meet his gaze without flinching, and said, "I'll do what I can."

But even as she said the words she knew that she would do more than just "what she could". She would do whatever it took. She wouldn't let Reid down, even if it meant transforming herself back into Sasha the Cat. Even if it meant working with him every day. Even if it meant resisting the temptation he represented.

Frankly, she didn't know what scared her more. The fear of letting him down or the fear of letting him get too close.

CHAPTER NINE

CHOOSING Jane to work on the *Trés Bien* pitch had seemed like a logical decision. After all, she really was better than anyone else at Forester+Blake when it came to sexy, innovative ideas.

Choosing to head up the project himself had also seemed logical. Reid had realized what he'd told Jane was true. And she just might be the one creative person at Forester+Blake that he was comfortable working with.

With Matt still pressuring him to work more with the creatives, working with Jane seemed like the perfect solution all around.

What he just didn't get was how two completely logical decisions had come back to bite him in the ass.

It was all he could do to keep his hands off her. She seemed to have no such problems. Ever since the day they'd spoken in his office, she'd been coolly polite, but distant.

He wished it didn't bother him, but it did. Getting involved with Jane was still a very bad idea. Never mind the thrill he got from just being with her. It was that same reckless glee that had gotten him into trouble so many times in the past. He was still her boss, and, for him, Forester+Blake would always come first.

And to make matters worse, he couldn't help wondering, did she want the real him or only the fantasy?

In the end, none of that mattered, because he still wanted her.

As he made his way to the conference room for the first of his meetings with Jane and Pete he tried to convince himself her disinterest was for the best. If she could maintain her distance, then so could he.

He'd been on the phone with a client, so he was the last to make it into the meeting. Audrey had been in earlier to set up a tray of cookies and muffins and to take everyone's coffee orders.

Seated throughout the room were the handful of other employees he'd invited to the meeting—the meeting which would show them just how wrong they'd been about Jane.

Reid noticed all of this as soon as he walked in the door, but it was Jane who captured and held his attention. She was at the front of the room fussing with some drawings set up on the easel. Ever since their pep talk the other day, she'd been coming to work dressed in a manner that was both provocative and professional. Very Sasha.

She wore her hair in the fussy style she seemed to favor lately. He actually would have preferred something a little more relaxed, but the way she was dressed made up for it. Today she wore a slim black skirt that ended several inches above her knees, paired with a vibrant red wraparound shirt that fastened with a bow just below her left breast.

As he settled into a chair at the far end of the conference table, he couldn't help staring at that bow on her blouse. Christmas presents had bows. Bright red ones, just like the one on her shirt.

Watching the presentation, he imagined what it would be like to unwrap Jane.

It'd be so simple. Tug on one of the ties and that bow would pull right apart. Peel back that fabric and there would be his present. Jane's fabulous breasts. Breasts he hadn't seen nearly enough of the night they'd almost had sex.

He struggled to concentrate on her words as she talked to the group about the strategy they'd come up with, but all he could think about was Jane's breasts. How they'd felt in his hands and how she'd arched into him, moaning deeply when he'd kissed them.

"So," Jane was saying as he tried, once again, to focus his attention on her words, "are there any questions before we show you what we've been working on?"

In the silence that followed, she looked at everyone in the room except him. Maybe he still made her nervous. Or maybe, like himself, she just had trouble concentrating when they were together.

After a pause, she continued. "As you all remember, we decided to build our pitch on the concept of anticipation."

Her words elicited a snort of derision from the asshole, but Jane sent him a look so dismissive and superior he quieted down.

"Since anticipation is—as they say—half the fun, our commercial will encourage women to wear *Trés Bien* lingerie as a way of building the anticipation for their—" she hesitated only an instant "—romantic encounters."

At her cue, Pete removed the cover sheet from the easel to reveal the artwork beneath.

The "shot" showed a man and woman together in a crowded elevator. The tagline below the drawing read: "If anticipation is half the fun…"

Another shot of the man and woman, the man leaning in to whisper something in her ear.

"If waiting for something makes you want it even more…"

The couple leaving the elevator. The doors closing behind them. Alone in the hotel hallway, they kiss.

"If knowing he wants you makes you want him even more…"

Inside the hotel room, the man removes the woman's jacket to reveal the *Trés Bien* bra underneath.

"Then what are you doing to build the excitement?"

By the time Pete showed the last of the pictures, the room was silent, the crowd clearly impressed by the work. It took a second for the spell to break. Then, one by one, people offered comments.

Reid said nothing. He kept his gaze focused on Jane, willing her to look at him, but her eyes didn't so much as dart in his direction. Obviously, she dreaded his reaction. And why wouldn't she? She'd just displayed their date for the whole office to see.

Oh, this time, she'd been more careful. Neither of the roughly sketched people in the drawings resembled either of them, but he'd have to be an idiot not to recognize the situation.

He tried to muster some indignation or anger. But he couldn't manage it. Seeing those pictures, he couldn't help but remember the events that had inspired them. The anticipation he'd felt standing beside Jane. The endless elevator trip up to her floor. The aching desire to pull her into his arms. To kiss her. To make her his, even though he knew he couldn't.

Worst of all, Jane made him reckless. And, in this case at least, she'd done it in front of some of his most important employees. All of whom, it seemed, were waiting to hear his opinion of the ad.

Matt had leaned forward and propped his elbows on the table. "Well, Reid, what do you think?"

He looked from one face to the next and saw the same thing in every expression. They all loved it.

Only Jane looked unsure. But now, at least, she was meeting his gaze. The uncertainty he saw in her eyes tugged at something deep inside him. He didn't have the heart to give her anything but praise. And that worried him, too.

"It's brilliant," he said, finally, as he shoved back his chair to stand. "I want to see a polished version by Wednesday. Pete, use whatever resources you need to make that happen. In the meantime, Jane, I want you to start working on a backup idea, just in case this one doesn't work out." To the rest of the group, he said, "We've still got a lot to do, so let's get back to work."

And then, because there were so many other things he wanted to say to her, but couldn't, he left the conference room.

Matt caught up with him just outside his office. "What was that all about?"

"I don't know what you mean."

"To start with, you were barely paying attention in there."

Reid shrugged out of his jacket and hung it on the coatrack just inside his office door. "I haven't been sleeping well."

Matt quirked his eyebrow. "Is that all it is?"

"What else could it be?"

Shrugging, Matt speculated. "I don't know…maybe a fight with that mysterious girlfriend of yours."

"There is no girlfriend," Reid insisted through clenched teeth.

Matt didn't look as if he believed him. "Speaking of the girlfriend, I noticed before the meeting that Jane wears the same perfume as your mysterious, non-existent girlfriend."

Damn it.

He considered his words before saying, "I'm not dating Jane, if that's what you're worried about."

Not dating her. Not sleeping with her. Not so much as touching her…unfortunately.

Matt studied him for a long minute before saying with a nod, "I brought it up only because it might not be a good idea—"

"Trust me," he interrupted. "I'm very aware of how stupid it would be to date Jane. I'm not an idiot."

Matt seemed to accept that answer, but—left alone in his office—Reid couldn't help wonder at all the half-truths he'd told Matt. There was no mysterious girl-friend, but that was Jane's perfume. He'd never taken Jane out on a date, but he'd nearly had sex with her. And, frankly, he didn't trust himself not to take her to bed if the opportunity ever arose again.

And then there was the greatest half-truth of all. He might not be an idiot, but—where Jane was concern-ed—he was certainly acting like one.

The illicit thrill of making a mistake with his eyes wide open. Of doing something he knew was wrong, but wanting her enough not to care.

It was the not caring that scared him. He worked hard to control his reckless streak. He didn't want this obsession with Jane to jeopardize Forester+Blake's success. But short of taking a long vacation until this was all over, he didn't see how to avoid it.

"B-brilliant?" Jane muttered the word like a curse as she stared down her reflection in the bathroom.

Brilliant? What the hell was that supposed to mean?

Brilliant had to be the least helpful bit of constructive criticism ever. Clearly Reid hated the idea. He'd looked bored to tears during the presentation and he'd told her to keep working on other ideas.

But if he hated it, why not point her in the right direction?

It had taken her half a day to screw up the courage to go ask Reid these questions, something the old Jane would never have considered doing. But Sasha would be bold. And if Sasha could do it, so could Jane.

She took one last assessing look at herself in the mirror before dropping her lipstick into her clutch purse and snapping it closed. Sasha makeup was in place…flawlessly applied by Dorothea this morning and then touched up over lunch. She wore her hair in the same shellacked, puffy mess she'd been wearing all week.

During the week she'd been dressing as Sasha, her career had taken a decided turn for the better. And, most miraculous of all, she had no stutter. Not even a hint of one. She spent every workday thinking like Sasha and acting like Sasha. As a result, every time she opened her mouth, she sounded like Sasha.

But the truth was, she was tired. So very, very tired of being Sasha. It was Friday night. The week had seemed interminable. All she wanted now was to go home, put on her pj's and climb into bed with a romance novel, a cat and a glass of wine.

But she couldn't do any of that until she talked to Reid.

Or could she?

What would happen if she went to him as Jane? No pretense, no personas. Just Jane.

She'd have to face him without Sasha's confidence. And she'd stutter, probably a lot. But was that really such a bad thing?

Sure, he was attracted to the way she looked when she was Sasha, but it wasn't as if he was going to sleep with her, no matter how she was dressed. So being Sasha when they were alone together gained her nothing.

But if she was going to face down Reid, she needed Sasha's confidence and strength. Sasha's confidence had abandoned her. She was also about to be alone with him again. Man, could she use a dose of courage right now.

She wanted—no, she needed—to walk into his office and demand answers from him. How could she do that if every time she opened her mouth, nothing came out?

She'd gotten more compliments—not just about her appearance, but about her work, as well. Everyone except Reid had gushed over the idea. He'd merely said, "It's brilliant," and stormed out. Okay, so he'd left. Stormed might be a bit of an exaggeration.

And could she blame him?

She was used to presenting her most intimate thoughts and ideas for others to pick apart and even she had been a little unnerved displaying her experiences with Reid.

It was only natural that he'd find the experience invasive.

Still, if he was going to nix the idea and send her

back to the drawing board, she'd rather know now. She inspected herself one last time in the mirror. She was one hundred percent Sexy Sasha, from the tips of her black pumps to the highest wisps of her big blonde hair.

Jane might quake in her boots at the thought of confronting Reid in his office, but Sasha merely licked her lips and grinned.

Still, Sasha was no dummy. She might not quake at the thought of confronting Reid, but she didn't want to do it in front of an audience, either. So as Jane left the women's restroom she looked carefully up and down the hall for signs of life from the cubicles. It was after seven on a Friday night, so everyone should be gone. Everyone except Reid, who never left work early.

His brusque, "Enter," did little to calm her nerves.

She nudged the door open and slipped into the room to find Reid seated, his chair turned to face the window. The overhead lights had been turned off, leaving only the lamp on his desk to light the room. She saw only his profile as he stared out at the Austin skyline. He was completely still except for the fingers of one hand, which tapped out a little tune on the armrest of his chair.

The scene was so much like something out of one of her fantasies that her breath caught in her chest and, for a moment, she couldn't speak.

"It's late," he said without even looking over his shoulder. "Go home to Angela. And no, I don't want to go to dinner with you, Matt. I'm not a charity case."

Momentarily disarmed, every ounce of Sasha vanished. "I w-wasn't going to invite you to dinner," she said, interrupting him before he got too far.

His fingers stilled. Then, slowly, he rotated the chair

to face her. In the dim lighting she could read little emotion in his shuttered expression.

"I wanted to talk to y-you about the pitch." She stepped into the room, allowing the door to close behind her.

"Go ahead."

She'd felt this way as a child the first time she'd jumped off the high dive. Nervous and unsure. Excited, but half convinced this would be the death of her. It had taken Jane all summer to muster the courage to jump. But Sasha would have taken the plunge on the first day of spring. Summoning that courage, Jane drew in a fortifying breath and jumped.

"I need to know what you thought of my idea." Her fingers clenched around her purse as a wave of nerves hit her squarely in the chest. She sucked in a deep breath and willed herself to relax. This situation wouldn't even faze Sasha.

"You couldn't guess?"

"If I could guess, would I need to come in here and ask?" she pointed out, letting a little of Sasha's sass shine through.

"No, I suppose not." His fingers began tapping again. "I said it was brilliant."

"That's what you said. But I wasn't sure that's what you meant."

"Okay, then—" he pushed back his chair and stood "—it's brilliant. Smart, sexy, and clever. It's exactly what they're looking for. Do you need me to keep going?"

The edge in his voice took her aback. "You're annoyed."

"No, I'm—" He broke off, sighed, and then ran a hand through his hair. "You put our date into a commercial. How did you think I'd feel?"

She shrugged. "I didn't…" But what could she say? She had put their date—moment by moment—into that ad. "It was the best idea I had." Surely he'd see that was what was important here. "If y-you hate it so much, you can always—"

"I'm not going to pull the presentation. You know that. It's too damn good."

Slowly the tension that had been knotting her gut all week began to dissolve. She'd been right, then. Reid's priorities were exactly what she'd expected. Company first, personal life second. She'd known he'd feel that way.

She'd known it, yet it still disappointed her. Fool.

"Okay, then," she said. "S-sorry to bother you." With a nod, she turned to leave. But at the door, she turned back. With a half laugh she admitted, "Today at the meeting, I would have sworn you w-weren't even paying attention."

"What?"

"You just seemed…I don't know, out of it, I guess."

"I was just, um…" he ducked his head sheepishly, his lips hinting at a smile "…calculating my taxes."

"Huh?"

For a second, she stood there dumbly, trying to make sense of his admission. Then the full implication of his words hit her.

"Oh."

He looked up at her and—despite the length of the room that separated them—she felt the heat of his gaze.

"Oh," she said again, flushed with embarrassment. "I had no idea. I'm so—"

"Don't apologize."

Suddenly the idea of leaving held no appeal. Or maybe it was just that her legs were too weak to carry her out.

She'd been fantasizing about Reid for five years. The idea that he was now fantasizing about her as well made her heart pound. And it gave her courage to do things she'd only ever dreamed of. It brought out her inner Sasha.

Moving into the room, she said, "I also wanted to ask you about those other ideas you wanted me to work on."

Caution gleamed in his eyes, but he said, "Ask away."

"The first ad was all about letting the anticipation build before a romantic encounter."

"Right."

She reached his desk and rounded the corner. "While lingerie is certainly useful for that, that's not the only reason a woman would want to wear great lingerie."

"It isn't?" His voice was low and rough.

"No." She stopped a few inches from him. Propping her hip on the edge of his desk, she stretched her legs out in front of her, mimicking a stance she'd seen him take many times. "Women often wear lingerie to boost their confidence."

"They do?"

"Sure." She'd half expected him to edge away from her, but he didn't move. "Lingerie is like a secret. Something you know that no one else does. For example, knowing that your stockings are being held up by a black lace garter belt—especially when it matches your black silk bra and panties? Well, that can give you a shot of courage."

Passion flickered in his eyes as his gaze drifted down her body. He swallowed visibly. "It can?"

His voice was like a caress, lowered and hoarse, yet smooth against her skin.

"Absolutely. When you know you have on sexy

lingerie, it can give you the courage to do something you've always wanted to do, but been afraid to."

"And you want to put this in a commercial?"

"Sure. Why not?"

"What is it the woman in the commercial wants to do but hasn't had the courage to?" he asked.

"It could be anything. Maybe she needs to give a big presentation at work. Maybe she needs the added confidence to impress her colleagues."

Jane straightened away from the desk and took a step towards him. Her heart was pounding in her chest with equal measures of fear and excitement. She let her fingers creep up the placket to toy with the top button of his shirt, even though they itched to rip the buttons from their holes and reveal the skin beneath. "Or maybe she really has the hots for her boss and is finally going to make her move."

She'd wanted this for so long, dreamed about it for years. She hardly dared to breathe while she waited for his response. What if he laughed at her? What if he sent her away?

Then again, what if he didn't?

CHAPTER TEN

REID covered Jane's hand with his. When he spoke, his voice was low and husky. "Maybe kissing her boss isn't such a good idea."

There was caution in his voice, but a spark of desire in his gaze. He wanted her. She could see it in his eyes. And he hadn't said no. That gave her the courage to press forward.

Her fingers squirmed out from under his to explore the patch of tanned skin left exposed at his neck. Finally, she looked up and met his gaze. His eyes had dilated, appearing black rimmed with just a hint of pale green. His expression was taut, with no trace of his easy crooked smile. "But her boss probably doesn't want to hurt her," he said.

His concern touched something deep inside of her, giving her a boost of confidence. He was such a good guy. Such a decent man. Sleeping with an employee? That was exactly the kind of thing decent, stand-up guys like Reid Forester never did.

But he wanted her enough he was actually considering it. That was the kind of power she—or rather, Sasha—had over him.

Man, oh, man. She'd been dreaming of this moment for the past five years. She'd be a fool to let the chance slip by. While she was a lot of things, stupid wasn't one of them.

Since he was still waiting for her response, she smiled—the kind of lip-smacking, self-satisfied smile women like Sasha always wore—and said, "Don't worry. That's not going to happen."

He swallowed visibly, as if just now realizing what he'd gotten himself into. "It's not?"

Her fingers crept down to his belt. "Nope. That's the beauty of her plan." She traced the brass with her fingertip, but didn't undo the buckle. "She's not planning on a relationship."

"She isn't?"

"Oh, no," she murmured, rubbing her palms across the fine cotton of his shirt, enjoying the way his muscles clenched deliciously beneath her touch. "This would definitely be a one-night stand kind of thing." She tugged his shirt free from his pants and made quick work of the few buttons that prevented her from truly enjoying his bare chest.

"You see," she went on, "she thinks a relationship would be too complicated, also. That's not what she wants."

"What does she want?"

Finally her fingers found his warm flesh. His stomach seemed to leap beneath her touch. For a moment, she was completely distracted by the sheer joy of touching him. By the shuttered, tense expression that flickered across his face as she touched him.

It seemed to take every ounce of strength he possessed to keep from touching her. But—thank good-ness—he was letting her run this show. The thought made her giddy with excitement.

She shook her head, trying to remember his question.

Oh, right. What was it she wanted? Him, completely at her mercy. Trembling. Begging. For her. Forever.

That thought stopped her cold.

Forever, she couldn't have. But tonight? She could have tonight.

"One unforgettable night."

Praying he couldn't hear the naked yearning behind her words, she twined her fingers through his hair and pulled his mouth down to hers.

Kissing Jane was reckless and stupid. Arguably the worst career move he'd ever made. But as he felt her lips part under his he didn't give a damn.

She tasted too good, too hot. And he felt as if he'd waited too long to feel her luscious body molded to his.

Her mouth was firm and hot under his. Her hands moving across his chest were delicate yet demanding. As desperate and needy as he was, yet somehow still in control. And her soft moan as he slipped his tongue into her mouth nearly drove him over the edge.

He felt her shoving his shirt off his shoulders, her hands clutching at his chest. The cool waft of the air-conditioning against his back contrasted sharply with the heat of her palms against his skin. She was like fire. Dangerous and exciting, yet destructive, as well.

Despite that, he couldn't stop touching her. Couldn't keep his hands away from the bow that held her shirt in place.

But before he could tug it loose, she wrenched her mouth from his. "No."

Instantly he stilled, though it took him a moment for his lust-befuddled brain to process the word. "No?"

Her lips curved into that sorceress's smile of hers and he nearly groaned in defeat.

"No," she repeated firmly. Smugly.

Before he could even ask a second time, she planted her hands on his chest and marched him backwards a step until his legs bumped against his chair. He barely resisted when she shoved at his shoulders, urging him to sit.

Her expression was an odd combination of desperation and control. Her lips moist and swollen. Her hair mussed from his fingers. She was the most erotic, sensual creature he'd ever seen.

How had he ever imagined he'd be strong enough to keep his hands off her?

He couldn't look at her and not ache to touch her.

Why not give himself what he so desperately wanted? As it was, wanting Jane had become a full-time occupation. Having her couldn't make that any worse. Once again he reached for the ties to her shirt, but she playfully swatted his fingers away.

Instead of letting him touch her, she stood just out of his reach. Her own fingers toyed with the bow on her shirt. Teased the ribbon, running it through her fingers, slowly loosening the knot with each pass down the length of its tail.

"Is this what you want?"

He nodded, but instead of untying the bow, she quirked an eyebrow and stilled. "Yes." The word tumbled out of his mouth.

She seemed completely in control. Only the rapid rise and fall of her chest revealed her heightened passion.

His heart pounded in his chest. As if he were a child at Christmas, unwrapping that first present, his anticipation all but boiled within him. He wanted desperately to see her. To touch her.

Still, she did nothing. So he added, "Please."

She smiled and with one firm tug the bow slipped free of its knot and her shirt gaped open. With a sexy little wiggle, she shook free of her shirt and dropped it to the floor.

Her breasts were encased in black silk and lace. Her skin seemed impossibly pale in contrast. Almost luminous in the half-light. Her nipples were hard, pressing against the fabric.

Aching to touch her, he started to stand. But she planted a hand on his shoulder. "No." She shook her head playfully, her expression one of teasing reprimand.

He would have thought her completely in control if he hadn't noticed the slight tremor in her fingers as she reached for the zipper on the side of her skirt. Every move she made was calculated to drive him mad. And it was working. His erection strained against his pants. He'd never wanted any woman more than he wanted Jane at this moment.

And then she shimmied out of the skirt with a seductive wiggle of her hips. She was dressed exactly how she'd described. Black bra and panties, black garter belt, sheer black stockings. Exactly how she'd described. But even his imagination hadn't done her justice.

"I'd almost convinced myself you couldn't possibly be as gorgeous as I was picturing you in my mind."

She stilled, waiting for him to continue.

"And I was wrong. You're more gorgeous. And whoever said anticipation is half the fun obviously never held you naked in his arms."

Her lips curved into a smile that was both alluring and mischievous at the same time. "Pretty sure of yourself, aren't you?"

Her tone was bold. Outrageous, given that she was all but naked and he was still partially dressed. But she held all the power here.

"Not sure," he admitted. "But hopeful."

Only then did she let him stand. Pulling him with her, she backed up against his desk and scooted onto the edge. She hooked her fingers through his belt loops and tugged him towards her, wrapping her stocking-clad legs around his.

She'd worked hard to hide her arousal. To keep things light and playful. But suddenly, there was desperation in her touch.

He groaned at the feel of her legs tightened around his hips. He kissed her neck, relishing the pounding of her pulse against his lips and the shuddering of her breath in her throat. As she trembled against him he found the clasp of her bra and flicked it open, releasing the weight of her full breasts into his hands.

Her nipples were hard against his palms. She groaned, arching her back so that her breasts thrust up to meet his touch. Her skin was impossibly silky and impossible not to taste.

He wanted to devour her. To absorb her completely.

As his mouth moved from one breast to the other he was only vaguely aware of her hands moving across his chest and then her fingers fumbling with his belt.

He felt her tensing as she struggled to undo the buckle. Felt her frustration mounting along with his own.

"Let me," he muttered.

"I've almost—"

Brushing her fingers away, he kissed her gently. "It's okay."

She bit down on her lip, her hands hot and eager at his waist while she waited for him to finish.

She seemed embarrassed by her awkwardness with his belt. The blush that crept into her cheeks implied an innocence that he found even more alluring than all her sexy lingerie.

That blush told him more clearly than she ever could that all her sexy bravado was for him and him alone. It pleased him that she obviously didn't make a habit of seducing men in their offices.

Mentally, he cursed as he remembered where they were. In his office. Of all the unromantic places to have sex with a woman for the first time… Of all the stupid, reckless ways he could screw up his career…

And yet, as he felt her hand enclose his erection, none of it mattered. Any thoughts of stopping her, of taking her home to his bed and making slow, lazy love to her where there was no risk of interruption or discovery, dissolved under the sweet, gentle pressure of her fingers.

Still he made himself offer. "Jane, wait…" he gasped as she scraped her fingernails down the length of his penis. He wrapped his hand around her wrist, forcing her to stop long enough for him to form a coherent thought. "Maybe we should wait. Go to my house. It's not far."

"No," she murmured, pressing her mouth to his. Her voice sounded husky and breathless. "Here. Now." She kissed him again, trailing her mouth to his neck while shoving his pants down with her free hand. "You have no idea how often I've imagined this. You and I, right here on this desk."

She met his gaze boldly, her eyes all but black in the half-light. For an instant, she seemed to flicker between the woman she was now and the "stranger" he'd met on the rooftop. Sasha. Exotic, sensual, bold, and enticing.

"I want this," she murmured.

"But—"

She pressed a finger to his lips. "Don't worry. If you want to take me home and do this all over again at your place, I won't complain."

Who was he to argue with a proposition like that?

Then she pulled a condom from God only knew where and tore the packet open, silencing any protests he might have made.

But even before her nimble fingers putting the condom on his erection drove him to distraction, he knew his protests were just for show. Nothing other than a protest from her could have stopped him.

Until he stepped back to look at her and saw the tiny scrap of fabric covering her mound. Bikini panties. Tied on either side with bows. His fingers trembled at he reached for the ribbon that dangled temptingly against her silky skin. With two quick tugs the bows dissolved and the last barrier between them fell to the floor.

She was so beautiful. So vulnerable. So completely his in this moment. The urge to drop to his knees and bow to her was almost overwhelming. And then she smiled at him. A tiny, almost shy smile that stripped away the last of his defenses.

He parted her thighs with a gentle reverence, aching as he stroked the delicate folds of her sensitive flesh. He found the nub of her desire and circled it with his thumb, watching her eyelids droop, her lips part in a gasp and her passion wash over her.

Her head dropped back and a low groan echoed through the room. "Please," she gasped. It was all the encouragement he needed, and he thrust into her.

When he felt the heat of her closing around him, he squeezed his eyes closed and bit back a groan.

He tried to hold back, to make the moment last. She made no such attempts. She arched against him, thrusting her hips up to meet his every move. Her legs wrapped around his hips, her rhythm guiding him. As he felt his arousal tighten and strain he opened his eyes, needing to see her. With her arms propped behind her, her breasts thrust up, her head arched back, she watched him through half-closed eyes.

She was an ancient pagan goddess come to life. Fertility, sexuality, and the most basic femininity.

He thrust into her one last time as his climax rocked through him. He felt her clench, her whole body convulsing around him as she called out his name.

Spent and barely able to stand, he nevertheless pulled her to him and cradled her against his chest. She felt right there, in his arms.

But as he held her and as the world slowly came back into focus, a vague sense of unease stirred within him.

Not because he'd done something incredibly stupid. Not because he'd been unbelievably reckless. At work, no less. Not because of any of the reasons he should have been feeling uneasy.

No, this was something deeper.

He'd just had sex with the most exotic, enticing woman he'd ever been with. Unfortunately, he wasn't quite sure who she was. Sasha, or Jane.

CHAPTER ELEVEN

AFTER six years in advertising, Jane knew as well as anyone that things seldom lived up to her expectations for them. The super-duper stain remover that left bleached splotches all over her clothes. The bargain vacation to Bermuda, during hurricane season, during a hurricane. The *Healthy Meals in Thirty Minutes* cookbook full of recipes that took over an hour to prepare, and which she'd gained ten pounds eating. Disappointments, one and all.

Reid Forester did not fall into that category.

In fact, sleeping with Reid Forester had exceeded her expectations so greatly, she was beginning to fear no other lover would measure up.

A risk she was willing to take, she'd decided at about three in the morning, when Reid had woken her and made slow, sleepy love to her before falling back asleep curled against her back.

When she woke a few hours later to find him still sleeping beside her, his hand curled around her breast, his breath warm on her neck, she knew she'd been right. The previous night was worth any cost.

But as she lay there, she couldn't help wondering what that price would be.

She shoved the thought aside to take in the details of his bedroom, as she hadn't bothered to the night before. Reid lived in one of the newer downtown condominiums. "Live downtown in luxury" was the building's tagline, if she wasn't mistaken. Despite the expensive price tag, Reid didn't appear to live luxuriously. His bedroom and living room—what she'd seen of it, anyway—were both furnished in reproduction mission-style furniture. Clean lines, no fuss, no-nonsense. Appealing in its simplicity and sheer masculinity.

The bedroom held just the bed, a single nightstand, a single wooden chair, and a chest of drawers, on top of which sat a collection of framed photos. Unable to resist the temptation to glimpse some tiny part of his life outside work, Jane slipped out from beneath his arm and padded across the plush carpet to the dresser.

All of the pictures were of Reid with his parents. Jane had met the Senior Mr. Forester several times during her first year on the job. Mrs. Forester she recognized from a company holiday party. The pictures were basic family stuff. A graduation photo of Reid looking young and exuberant, his arm slung around his mother's shoulder. The family in front of a Christmas tree.

What had he been like as a kid? Rebellious or an overachiever? She couldn't help wishing she'd known him then. Hell, she couldn't help wishing she knew him now.

"Keep dreaming," she told herself. Shaking her head, she made her way to the bathroom.

But in the bathroom, she stopped stone-still to stare in horror at the reflection in the mirror.

Last night, Reid Forester had gone to bed with Sasha, but this morning he was going to wake up with Jane.

The eye makeup Dorothea had carefully applied

over twenty-four hours ago was now smeared in dark streaks under her eyes. Her skin appeared pale and splotchy. But her hair was the worst. Her hair—which last night had been curly, big, and beautiful—was now a flattened mat of tangles. Except for the occasional odd spiky chunk. And she didn't know how to fix any of this.

This was a code-red emergency.

She glanced down at her watch. Just after eight. Without knowing what time Reid normally woke on a Saturday morning, she had to assume she didn't have much time.

She cracked open the bathroom door and peered into his bedroom. Lying on his back, one arm stretched over his head, the sheet rumpled at his hips, Reid looked like a sex god. All lean muscle and scruffy day-old beard.

For an instant she was tempted. Screw her appearance. What did it matter? She could crawl back into bed with him and do something so positively wicked he'd never notice what she looked liked.

Except that he would notice what she looked like. He was a guy. And everybody knew men were visually stimulated.

If she crawled into his bed looking like this, chances were the only thing she'd stimulate was his fight-or-flight instinct.

Okay, if she didn't want him seeing her like this, option two was fixing it somehow. The bad news was, she had yet to successfully style her hair on her own.

Scanning the bedroom, she spotted her purse lying discarded on a chair near the bed. Barely daring to breathe, she tiptoed across the room, snagged her purse and crept back to the bathroom.

A few minutes later, she had Dorothea on the phone. "What the hell do I do with it?"

"With what, dear?" Dorothea asked calmly.

"My hair," she snapped into the phone. "I look like Alfalfa. Y-you've got to help me!" She heard an odd sound through the phone. "Are y-you laughing?"

"Of course not," Dorothea murmured soothingly. "Do you want me to come over and fix it?"

Come to Reid's? Yeah, that'd be subtle. He'd never doubt she was the confident, sophisticated woman she was pretending to be if she needed her friend to come do her hair for her.

"No," she told Dorothea. "I'm not at home."

"Really?" Dorothea's voice rose with glee. "Oh, good for you! Well done."

"No, n-not well done." Staring at herself in the mirror, she plucked at one of the errant strands. "N-not if he sees me looking like this."

This time, Dorothea definitely chuckled. "Okay, I'll try to talk you through it. Just remember, the way you style your hair is for you as much as it is for him."

"Wh-what's that supposed to mean?"

"The hairstyle gives you confidence, not beauty."

"Thanks," she snapped, too panicked to keep the sarcasm from her voice.

Dorothea ignored her sarcasm and quipped, "You're welcome. First off, have you tried brushing it?"

"No." Jane looked around the bathroom but didn't see a brush out on the counter. Feeling only a bit guilty for invading his privacy, she yanked open the drawer and rummaged for a brush.

When she found one, she ran it through her hair. "It's not helping," she complained.

"Try wetting it."

Jane set down the phone, splashed water on her hair, and then assessed her reflection. The rebellious strands were now back under control. Breathing out a sigh of relief, she picked the phone back up. "Okay, it's not sticking up anymore. What next?"

"Now just reapply some sculpting lotion and blow it dry like I've been showing you."

"Sculpting lotion? You didn't say I'd need any sculpting lotion."

"Darlin', I'm saying it now, aren't I?" The hint of East Texas twang was a sure sign she was getting annoyed.

"I'm sorry. It's just…I don't have any sculpting lotion."

"Hair spray?"

"No…wait, let me check." She pawed through her purse. "I've got a tube of lipstick, powder, Juicy Fruit gum, a condom, and my wallet."

"Not even MacGyver could fix your hair with that."

"Hold on, I'll keep looking."

She looked through the drawer, but found only a toothbrush and toothpaste. The cabinet by the sink yielded a bottle of cologne and a can of shaving cream, but no hair-care products.

"No. Nothing. Wh-what am I going to do?"

"Have you considered just letting him see you as you are now?"

Let him see the real Jane? The Jane he'd ignored for five years? Not on her life.

"Never mind," she told Dorothea. "I'll figure something out on my own. But thank you."

She hung up and tossed the phone back into her bag. What a disaster.

Biting down on her lip, she withdrew the bottle of

cologne. She sprayed a squirt into the air and inhaled deeply. The familiar woodsy scent nearly made her knees give out.

Maybe Dorothea was right, but was that a chance she was willing to take?

After all, Reid had never noticed her before her transformation into Sasha.

She cracked the door open and peeked out. He was still asleep. If she had anything to with it, he'd never have to see her as she really was.

"Ah, Jane, where the hell are you?"

Reid stared at the note she'd left for him for a long moment, then tossed it aside, flopping onto his back.

Funny, the image of her neat handwriting seemed burned in his mind. "Sorry to run, just remembered an appointment. Call when you get up."

And she'd left a phone number. If he had to guess, her cell phone, since it was different from the home number listed in her file at work.

The fact that he knew that disturbed him. He shouldn't have looked up her home number last week. He shouldn't have—consciously or not—committed it to memory. Both of which were relatively minor sins when put in the bigger picture, but it rattled him nevertheless.

Jane was quickly becoming an obsession.

He sat up, scrubbed a hand down his face, then swung his legs over the side of the bed. He wouldn't call her. Not yet, at least.

If she could sneak out without so much as waking him to say goodbye, then he could damn well wait until tomorrow to call her.

But as he pulled on his jeans, he remembered she'd once accused him of wanting her only because he couldn't have her.

If he didn't call her until tomorrow, would she think she'd been right? That he didn't want her anymore now that they'd slept together?

Okay, he wouldn't wait until tomorrow. He'd call her after lunch.

But as he tugged a T-shirt over his head he remembered how endearingly embarrassed she'd been about fumbling with his belt buckle. What an intriguing contradiction she was. One minute, confident and bold. The next, vulnerable and diffident.

If he didn't call until the afternoon, would she think she'd done something wrong?

He pressed the heel of his palm against his forehead and groaned.

Before he could talk himself out of it, he'd picked up the phone. As he dialed the number he glanced down at his watch. Twelve minutes.

He'd gone from waiting until tomorrow to call her to waiting twelve minutes. Brilliant.

"Why'd you leave?" he asked almost as soon as she answered.

"I had an appointment," she said a little too quickly. "Didn't you get the note? Of course you got the note. You w-wouldn't have had my number otherwise." She laughed nervously.

He lowered himself to the foot of his bed and propped his elbows onto his knees. "I was looking forward to taking you to breakfast," he admitted, staring at the carpet between his bare feet. "Sweetish Hill Bakery is just around the corner. They make great pastries."

She was silent for a long moment and he heard the sounds of traffic in the background, which meant she was still in her car. Apparently, he'd just missed her.

Finally she said, "Sorry I missed it."

"Are you free tonight?"

"Why?"

Why? God, she was a strange one. "I thought I'd take you to dinner."

"The River City Grill?" she teased.

"Actually, I was thinking of Botinita's. It's a little Mexican place down on South First. It's a real dive. Great food. Spicy. You'll love it."

Again she hesitated. He could almost hear her weighing her answer. "I'm busy for dinner. But I could come by your place afterwards. Around ten?"

"How about tomorrow night, then?"

"Sorry."

"What about lunch?"

"Mmm...still busy."

Drinks? Brunch? High tea? He was tempted to offer, but didn't. He knew what she'd say. Busy, busy, and busy.

Either Jane had the most active social calendar of any woman he'd ever met, or she was avoiding him. Outside of bed, that was.

"What about tonight?" she asked. "Do you want me to come by?"

It was crazy. Clearly, she didn't want anything to do with him outside the bedroom. Just another complication in a relationship that was already way too complicated. It would be so much easier to just end this now.

"Sure," he heard himself say. "Around ten."

* * *

At 10:08, Jane sat in her car—parked in the visitor's spot outside Reid's condo—forehead pressed to the steering wheel.

They'd agreed to just one night. So why did he want to see her again? And why had she said yes? Could she handle another night without doing something stupid like falling in love with him?

Yes, she could handle it. She'd never expected this to last forever. She'd wanted one great night. Anything beyond that was part of the bonus round, right?

She sat up and flipped down the visor mirror to check her makeup. She'd spent all day with Dorothea practicing applying her makeup and styling her hair. She'd washed, dried, and styled it three times, until she could recreate Dorothea's creation.

Now, she looked impeccable. One hundred percent Sasha. One hundred percent the sexy woman Reid expected on his doorstep.

Except Sasha wouldn't give a damn about getting too involved. Hell, for that matter, no man would dare reject Sasha. It simply wouldn't happen, because Sasha would be totally in control of every relationship. Totally in control.

With renewed determination, she thrust open the door to her car and climbed out. She repeated the words like a mantra as she waited for him to buzz her through at the street-level door. By the time she rang his doorbell, she almost even believed them.

When he opened the door, he looked so handsome, she had to remind herself again. Sasha didn't get emotionally involved. It didn't matter how unbelievably handsome the man was.

And Reid was unbelievably handsome. So much so that he took her breath away.

He was dressed in blue jeans and a green T-shirt. The exact color of his eyes. The shirt was untucked. The jeans faded in all the right spots. His feet were bare.

The simple intimacy of his bare feet made her heart pound. She could picture him padding barefoot around the kitchen, making coffee on a Sunday morning. Or stretched out on the sofa watching a DVD on a lazy Saturday afternoon, his bare feet rubbing against hers, their legs intertwined as she lay sprawled across his chest, mercilessly distracting him from the movie.

Before she could melt into a puddle on his front doorstep, he tugged her inside, shut the door behind her and pulled her to him.

Cradling her face in his hands, he kissed her soundly. Slowly. And with excruciating thoroughness.

Her blood pounded in response. For a moment, she could barely remember her own name, let alone that she was supposed to be controlling this.

Finally, he released her mouth, nuzzling his nose against hers as he pulled away.

"I wasn't going to kiss you," he said.

"You weren't?" she asked, her voice sounding as breathless and weak as she felt.

"No." He tugged on her hand to pull her further into the condo. "I was going to politely invite you in. Offer you a drink. Ask about your day."

"Why didn't you?"

He flashed her a smile. One of the crooked half-smiles that did terrifying things to her insides. "You looked too good. I couldn't help myself."

"And now?"

"And now…would you like to come in? Have a drink?"

"Sure," she said weakly.

With his hand warm and strong on her back, he guided her out of the entryway and into the living room. Last night, he'd barely turned on the lights as he'd led her to the bedroom. This morning, she'd been too preoccupied to notice much. Now, waiting for him to return with her drink, she looked around. She didn't want to be nosy, but how could she resist?

Like his bedroom, the furniture in this room sported clean lines. A leather sofa and vintage club chair, a flat-screen TV with all the accompanying paraphernalia. On the floor beside the TV sat the latest gadget from PlayStation, with half a dozen video games. A shelf nearby stored a collection of DVDs. One that overlapped quite a bit with her own collection. Over the fireplace hung four framed cells from Warner Brothers' cartoons. Elmer Fudd, Daffy Duck, the Tasmanian Devil, and—of course—Marvin the Martian.

When he returned from the kitchen, she was running her finger along the spines of his DVDs.

"Most of those were my mother's," he said, holding out a glass of red wine. "When she passed away a couple years ago, I couldn't bear to get rid of them. She loved watching movies."

She wanted to ask more about his mother, but resisted the temptation.

Figured. The one thing they had in common and they didn't really have it in common at all. She accepted the glass. "I did wonder about *Anne of Green Gables*."

"Which one?" he asked, not even recognizing the title.

She extracted the DVD from its slot and held it up. He glanced at it, then smiled. "Oh, that. It's a classic."

"Never seen it, have you?"

"Nope."

She slid the case back onto the shelf with a sigh. "And the games? Were those your mother's, too?"

He laughed. "Purely research. You never know when they're going to put out a request for proposals. I just want to be prepared."

And that seemed to say it all. She was classic, romantic movies, he was testosterone-driven video games. Worlds apart, in so many ways.

Disconcerted by the thought, she sidled away from him to stand before the fireplace and pretended to study the framed photos of him and his parents that sat on the mantel.

"That was taken on our first family vacation." He pointed to a shot of them on a ski trip, bundled into parkas, skis in hand.

Reid appeared to be about sixteen, lean and rangy. His eyes narrowed with teenage rebellion not even a family vacation could banish.

"Your *first* family vacation?" she asked, searching his face for some sign he was teasing her. She laughed nervously. "I mean, I've heard about the Forester family work ethic, but no family vacations? That's ridiculous. You've gotta be, what? Fifteen, sixteen in this picture?"

"Fifteen." For a moment he merely stared at the picture, his shoulders slightly hunched and his hands shoved deep into his pockets. Then he slanted her a smile. "It wasn't Dad's first vacation in fifteen years. It was just our first vacation after they adopted me. I was still in my angry and rebellious stage. We went skiing over spring break. Up in Colorado. I'm lucky they didn't leave me there."

He rambled on a bit about the lodge they stayed at, but when he noticed her staring at him in surprise, he broke off. "You didn't know."

"That you were adopted?" She shook her head. "No, I didn't." Then, after a second, she chuckled. "I guess it makes sense, though. With all the *pro bono* work the firm does for adoption groups."

"Actually, it's the other way around. Dad was doing the *pro bono* work when he stumbled across me. I was in a group home up near Waco when he came by to film an ad for the Texas Adoption Council."

"A group home?" she asked. "Like an orphanage?"

Her shock must have shone through in her voice, because he chuckled wryly. "Nothing quite so Dickensian."

She raised her eyebrows in disbelief.

"It wasn't so bad. Better than at some of the foster homes I stayed in."

Which, she knew, wasn't saying much. She'd watched enough *60 Minutes* and *20/20* in her lifetime to know that sometimes life in the foster-care system was no day at the beach. Still, his voice held none of the resentment or anger she might have expected.

"I was fourteen at the time, but kids that old never get adopted. But I figured, the younger kids, they still had a shot. Whenever anyone would come by the home, I'd try to sell the younger kids. Talk about how smart and well behaved they were."

She couldn't help but laugh at the image of a young Reid trying to hawk children like used cars.

"I knew the crew was just there to film the spot," he

went on, "but I figured it couldn't hurt. The next weekend, he came back and he brought his wife. There was this real cute freckled kid—maybe nine or ten. I was sure I'd sold them on him. But it was me they wanted."

Even now, all these years later, she heard a hint of disbelief in his voice. That blatant vulnerability tugged at something deep in her heart. Something real and far more complicated than the simple sexual fantasies she was used to.

"They must have loved you very much."

"Hmm, maybe. Dad used to say he just hadn't been able to resist someone who was a such natural adman."

"Is that why you never told your father you didn't want to run Forester+Blake?"

He turned sharply to study her. "How do you know that?"

Suddenly, she felt very aware of him. He stood so close to her, yet didn't touch her. His mere proximity made her senses reel and her skin tingle. She felt herself sway closer to him. But instead of kissing her, as she hoped he would, he seemed to be waiting for her to say something. To answer his question, she realized.

"What? That you never wanted to run Forester+Blake?" She held his gaze for only a moment longer before returning her attention to the photos on the mantel. "You just don't seem to love it, I guess. You take it all so seriously. Matt's not like that. Your father wasn't like that." He stiffened and she felt him withdraw from her. So she added, "Maybe you should try to have more fun with it."

"That seems to be a popular opinion these days."

There was a wry, self-deprecating quality in his voice, but a tightness, as well. She'd offended him.

"I didn't mean—"

"I know what you meant. And you're right. I don't love it. But it's my job. Forester+Blake is my responsibility. It's what I've worked for ever since the Foresters adopted me."

"But it's not what you've always planned to do. If they didn't adopt you until you were fifteen, then before they came along you must have had some idea what you wanted to do with your life. Some plan for the future. Maybe you could—"

"Before the Foresters adopted me, I was in and out of trouble my whole life." He spoke quietly and without emotion. But she heard the hurt behind his words. Saw it in the tilt of his chin and the sadness of his gaze. "I'd been in fights. I'd been arrested at least half a dozen times. I'd been suspended from school too often to count and I'd been in more foster homes than I remember. Before they came along, I had no future. So what I wanted to do with it is irrelevant."

She ached for that troubled boy he'd been. A boy with no future. And she ached to pull him into her arms, hold him close to her, and whisper to him that it was okay for him to dream again.

Unable to say all the things she wanted to, she said, "Your father was very proud of you."

For a moment, he said nothing, but his mouth twisted into a doubtful frown. "You think?"

Her heart tightened at the vulnerability in his voice. "He talked about you all the time." Desperately wanting him to believe her, she touched his arm, waiting for him to meet her gaze before continuing. "About how smart and clever you were. How hard you worked in college. His son, Reid, who was off getting his MBA at

Stanford. That's the way he said it, with his voice just booming with pride."

That was when it hit her. Her fascination with Reid had started long before she'd ever met him. It had started back in her earliest days at Forester+Blake, listening to the senior Mr. Forester brag about his son.

She'd been just twenty-one, fresh out of college, when she'd been hired on at Forester+Blake. It was the only job she'd ever had. The only one she'd ever wanted. Still, she'd been fascinated by Reid, who'd begun his MBA at Stanford not long before she was hired. Even then he'd been almost legendary for his hard work and his hard play. Rock climbing in Utah. Kayaking in Costa Rica. Scuba diving off the coast of British Columbia. It was all so daring and adventurous.

She'd never had a chance, really. She'd been primed to fall in love with Reid before she'd even met him.

Not that she was in love with him now, she reassured herself. This was just lust. Puppy love gotten out of hand. Mixed with respect. And this weird, inexplicable protective urge. And, sure, maybe the slightest hint of affection thrown into the mix.

Oh, no.

She felt a sinking sensation in her belly.

This was bad. This was very bad.

She was in way over her head.

After all, this was short term. That was what they'd agreed upon. She was having enough trouble getting her body to remember that without complicating matters by getting her heart involved, as well.

"What about your parents?" Reid asked.

"Huh?" It took a second for her attention to snap back to the moment.

"Are they proud of you?"

"Oh, I don't know… I guess Mom is. I'm financially independent and that's huge with her. I think as long as I'm regularly contributing to my personal retirement plan, she's proud."

"What about your dad?"

"I don't know. We never talk about it." She laughed at the irony. "Actually, we never talk about anything. My dad's pretty much a birthday- and Christmas-card kind of guy. I don't think I'd even get those if it wasn't for Christine."

"Christine?"

"Wife number three. The overachiever. Before she came along, my sisters and I hadn't heard from him in years."

"Your parents divorced?"

She nodded, but couldn't quite find the words to talk about it.

"That must have been hard," he murmured.

He was watching her so closely. Really listening to her. So many times she'd imagined being the center of his attention, but she'd never imagined it like this. Talking about her parents' divorce. Dredging up all those awful memories. All the fighting. Then her father's abrupt—but permanent—absence from their lives.

"Tell me about it."

She looked up at him, surprised. "You don't really want to—"

"Yes, I do. I really want to hear about it."

He had that tenacious, determined gleam in his eyes. She sighed, knowing he probably wasn't going to let this go, so she made as light of it as she could. "After Dad moved to Florida, Mom got a job at Texas Instruments and worked a lot. Elizabeth, my oldest sister, decided that meant she was in charge. So she spent most of her time bossing everyone around. And Katie, my little sister, just turned into a rebellious hellion. She used to—"

"What about you?" he interrupted her to ask.

"Me?"

He brushed a lock of hair from her eyes. "Yeah, you."

Her stutter had gotten much worse, exacerbated by her mother's growing impatience and by her sisters' outrageous behavior. There had been times, in fact, when it had seemed easier not to speak at all. So she hadn't. For days at a time, sometimes. Once for more than a week.

None of which she wanted to share with him. So she shrugged. "I got by."

He continued to watch her, his expression making it clear he knew there was more to her story. "So if your older sister was the bossy one and your younger sister was the rebellious one, which one were you?"

"I was the quiet one, I guess. I just sort of slipped under everyone's radar and tried not to get caught in the crossfire."

Then, suddenly, it occurred to her how absurd it was for her to be complaining about all of this to him. Given his past, her family angst seemed petty and a little pathetic, so she hastily tacked on, "Hey, don't get me wrong. It wasn't that bad. My mother, sisters and I are really close now. We get together when we can for holidays and stuff."

"Do they all live up in Dallas?"

She slanted him a look of surprise. "My mother and older sister live there. How'd you know that?"

"You mentioned it when we met on the roof. And—" he ducked his head as if embarrassed "—your personal file at work lists an Elizabeth Demeo of Highland Park as your emergency contact."

"You looked in my personal file?" she asked, incredulous.

He shrugged, his lips curving into an impish smile that did very naughty things to her insides. "What can I say? You make me weak."

At his words, her stomach seemed to drop clear to the floor. She made him weak.

How many times in her fantasies had she imagined him saying that exact thing to her? How many times had she imagined him looking at her like that, in that heated, hungry way of his? With the mischievous smile and the knowing glint?

Hundreds? Thousands? Countless, certainly.

And yet…and yet he wasn't really saying those words to her. It wasn't Jane Demeo who fascinated him. Who piqued his curiosity and made him weak. It was Sasha.

For five years he hadn't been the least bit interested in Jane, but one evening with Sasha had him violating company policy.

In short, Sasha made him weak. Jane just made him money.

CHAPTER TWELVE

STANDING just behind Jane, Reid ran his hand up her arm to her shoulder, brushing aside her hair in a gesture that was disturbingly familiar.

Her stomach flipped over at his touch. She leaned into the caress as the heat of sensual promise swirled through her body to pool between her legs and a whimper of longing stirred in the back of her throat.

But what was it she longed for? The raw pounding heat of sexual gratification, or the simple pleasure of a lazy Saturday afternoon watching DVDs?

Sasha would have stayed in control. Would have sidestepped these emotionally dangerous minefields. But how would she have done it?

With sex, of course.

And sexual gratification was so much easier than all these emotions tripping her up.

Jane let her eyes drift closed and allowed the sensations she'd been trying to keep at bay to flood over her. Reid standing so close behind her. His fingers on her neck. His heat and scent filling the air. The memory of his powerful reaction to her the previous night.

Sasha had tremendous power over this man. *She* had power over him.

Slowly she turned to face him. They both still held glasses of wine, so she took his into her other hand and then set them both on a nearby end table.

Wrapping her arms around his neck and pressing her body to his, she murmured, "I can only stay a couple of hours. You don't really want to spend them talking about my family, do you?"

Triumph pulsed through her as she felt his body's response to her actions—the tightening of his muscles, the quick intake of breath, the subtle throbbing of his penis against her belly.

Her satisfaction dipped when he untwined her arms from around his neck and distanced himself from her. "Actually, I thought we might have some dessert."

"Dessert?"

He pointed to the coffee table, where, she noticed for the first time, sat a take-out box, a napkin and a couple of forks.

"I got takeout from Sweetish Hill." Grabbing her hand, he pulled her around the coffee table to sit on the sofa. He popped open the box and displayed it proudly. "Chocolate-mousse cake and a strawberry tart."

She nearly closed her eyes and groaned. Chocolate-mousse cake? How could she resist?

"And you haven't tried the wine yet," he pointed out. "I could build a fire in the fireplace."

She shifted in her seat to face him, pulling her leg up onto the sofa and tucking it under her. "A fire? It's nearly seventy out."

"I can bump down the air conditioner," he reasoned.

His arm stretched out along the back of the sofa to

toy with her hair. To mess with her senses and keep her off balance.

The wine, the dessert, the fireplace, they made her want to give in. To give up control. And she was tempted—oh, so tempted. It was all so romantic.

But that was the problem. It was all so romantic.

She could imagine it in perfect detail. In an instant, the full-blown fantasy popped into her head. Not of sex and Reid, but of romance and Reid. Spending the rest of the evening curled up on the sofa with him, sipping the wine, feeding each other bites of cake and strawberry tart, watching the fire or maybe popping in one of the DVDs. Something scary so that she could curl against him and hide her face against his chest.

Much more thinking like that and soon she'd be imagining waking up in his arms and actually going to breakfast with him. And just like that, the image popped into her head. The two of them seated at one of the outdoor tables at Sweetish Hill, cups of coffee steaming on the table between them, nibbling on hot croissants as they read the Sunday paper, a dog lying at their feet, its leash tied to one of the chairs.

She stiffened, jerking away from Reid's touch as well as from the image.

He didn't have a dog. She sure as hell didn't have a dog. So where the hell had the dog come from?

She was a cat person, for cripes' sake.

Panic hit her hard in the belly as she realized what she'd done. She'd just imagined getting a dog with Reid.

Getting a dog was a long-term commitment. Dogs lived, like, fifteen years or something.

This was bad. Very. Very. Bad.

Sharing childhood secrets was bad enough.

Sharing pets was out of the question. She had to regain control.

She took a long drink of her wine—which she barely tasted—then set aside the glass. She ran a hand up the front of his shirt, relishing the feeling of lived-in cotton beneath her fingertips. "Dessert sounds good," she practically cooed. "But you know what I really want for dessert?"

He studied her, his expression blank, and for a moment she wondered if she'd overplayed her hand. Then he shook his head. "No. What?"

She ran a sculpted fingernail down the length of his jaw to his chin. "You."

Before he could respond, she set aside his wineglass and climbed onto his lap. Straddling his hips, she brought her mouth down to his.

She poured everything into that kiss. All of her need, but all her frustrations, as well. Her frustrations with herself and her stubborn, intractable imagination, and her frustration with him, for making this so damn hard on her.

Why couldn't he have followed the rules? Played the game the way she'd expected him to? Didn't he know this was about sex, not romance? Why was he ruining this for her?

As if to punctuate her thought, he wrenched his mouth out from under hers, pushing her gently away from him. "Wait, Jane—"

"No." She cuffed his wrists in her hands and pressed them back into the sofa. "I've waited all day for this." She kissed him again, trailing her lips across his mouth, to his ear. His skin was hot beneath her lips and tasted of raw masculinity and of passion. Of everything she'd ever wanted and never thought she could have. Of heated late-night dreams and early-morning fantasies.

Touching him made her heart pound and flesh pulse. Kissing him made her ache.

Rubbing the apex of her legs against his growing erection, she murmured, "I've thought about you all day. Wanted this all day."

It felt good to say it aloud. The admission thrilled her, kicking up a notch the desire already pushing against her restraint. There were a thousand other things she wanted to say to him that she didn't dare utter, so she pressed her mouth to his, pouring her emotions into a kiss that was deep and dark and full of secrets.

He easily could have overpowered her, but he didn't. He let her have her way with him. Still, her control was only an illusion. In truth, even while acquiescing, he filled her. Dominating her senses and sapping her will-power.

Desperate to regain some of her control, she released one of his wrists to trail her hand down his chest to his abdomen. "You want this, too. I know you do."

Grinding her mouth against his, she sought the waistband of his jeans with her fingers. The skin of his belly was hot and hard. She felt his muscles clench in response to her touch, felt his resistance weaken and then give beneath her onslaught.

She felt a surge of satisfaction at his surrender. Pure feminine power. Their coupling was faster, more impatient than before. They tugged restlessly at clothes. She yanked his T-shirt up and over his shoulders, but got his jeans and boxers only partway down his legs.

He pulled her dress over her head, but managed to

only shove the straps of her bra down her shoulders without unfastening the clasp.

As her trembling fingers struggled to ease the condom down the length of his penis, he merely shoved aside her panties. He rubbed her clitoris with the pad of his thumb, making her shiver with pleasure and ache with need.

His mouth rose up to meet hers and his tongue rubbed against hers. She found her control slipping away from her. With every touch, the balance of power slipped infinitesimally in his direction, until, suddenly, he was controlling the kiss.

Desire pounded through her veins, making her desperate. Frantic. Needy.

She struggled to hang on, clinging to the last shreds of her control. But his touch was relentless. Every stroke brought her closer to the edge. She squeezed her eyes closed, only to be flooded with images from every fantasy she'd ever had of him. Her control slipped away and her orgasm rocketed through her.

Then he was thrusting up into her, anchoring his hands on her waist. She rocked her hips forward, increasing the pressure that built within her. Hands braced on his shoulders, back arched, and eyes closed, she rode him to the crest of her passion.

He thrust up into her one last time, his hands convulsing on her hips, his eyes squeezed closed, his expression taut with ecstasy as he groaned her name. As she felt the last surge of his passion she ground herself down onto him, clenching around him, her eyes drifting closed, his name a percussive force in her mind that never quite made it to her lips.

As the last waves of her orgasm washed over her

body, she allowed herself to relax against his chest. In that instant, she felt as if she really were Sasha.

Then, slowly, her satisfaction gave way to a burgeoning sense of dread. She'd completely lost control, which Sasha never would have done.

Worse still, if Sasha always controlled her relationships, it meant she would have to be the one to end her relationship with Reid.

She felt a prickling of moisture at her eyelids that she refused to acknowledge as tears.

If she was going to end it with Reid, she'd have to do it soon. While she still had the strength to.

For the second morning in a row, Reid woke up alone. This time, at least, he'd been prepared for it.

Last night, Jane had made no bones about not intending to stay. She had—in fact—waited all of three minutes before climbing off his lap and dressing. She'd given him a final kiss before leaving, but she'd given no signs of even being tempted to stay. Not even by the chocolate-mousse cake. Not even a little.

Which, frankly, annoyed him. Not only was she able to resist him, she'd resisted the whole package— the wine, the fire, the chocolate. Women were supposed to live for all that.

Not that the sex itself wasn't great, because it was. Mind-blowingly great. And not just on his end, either. He'd felt her climax hard on the heels of his own. He'd felt her shivering in his arms, her muscles weakened by the force of her response. And seconds later she'd up and walked away.

What had gone wrong?

And why was it that the more time he spent with her,

the more off balance he felt? And what had happened to all his careful resolve to maintain his distance? After all, she was still an employee. So why wasn't he treating her like one?

Women were supposed to get less mysterious, not more mysterious. He could only conclude that Jane was unlike any woman he'd ever known. More dangerous and more intriguing.

So Sunday morning, determined to kick this thing once and for all, he stopped by Whole Foods for fresh flowers and pastries, then drove down to the south side of town to her little bungalow. He pulled to a stop a few doors down, but didn't get out of the car.

Maybe he should just let it go. So she wanted their relationship to stay purely sexual. So what? That was what they had first agreed on and most men would be satisfied with that.

And he might be, too, if he didn't know her better. If he didn't sense that sexual aggression hid some deeper emotion she kept carefully buried.

He'd almost talked himself into going up and ringing her doorbell when her door opened and she came out.

He watched from a few doors down as she juggled her bags while struggling to lock her door behind her. She was dressed simply, in jeans and a T-shirt. Her honey-blonde hair was pulled back into a ponytail and covered by a ball cap, except for a few strands that had slipped free around her face. The difference in her appearance intrigued him. She looked so much more natural, so much more comfortable than she did when she was dressed up for work. Yes, at work, she looked sexy as hell, but here she looked relaxed. He'd never seen this side of her before, and somehow it was even more appealing.

He was so entranced by her, it took him a minute to notice what she was carrying out to her car. She had a cooler in one hand, a backpack slung over one shoulder, and two long skinny bags over the other shoulder. The kind of bags designed to hold folding camp chairs.

What was she doing? Going on a picnic?

He did another mental catalogue of her bags.

She *was* going on a picnic.

With someone else.

Two chairs meant two people. And she sure as hell hadn't invited him on a picnic.

Reid's hands clenched around the steering wheel as emotion flooded him. Equal parts indignation and jealousy swept through him as he watched Jane load her bags into the trunk of her car. Before he knew what he was doing, he was following her as she headed west on Barton Springs Road.

Looked as if she was going to Zilker Park—maybe even the Botanical Gardens—right down by the river.

His indignation kicked up a notch. With him, she wouldn't even drink a single glass of wine. Wouldn't eat a bite of chocolate cake. But with some other guy, she'd go on a romantic picnic at the Botanical Gardens?

But before he could get himself too worked up, a couple of blocks before the gardens, she turned north.

He let his foot ease off the accelerator. Okay. Not the gardens.

His mind scrambled to come up with a romantic picnic site just north of the river, but hadn't come up with any by the time she turned again, this time onto a smaller side road that curved along beside soccer fields and a series of low gray buildings.

Was she going to watch some other guy play soccer?

That seemed odd. Especially since the only people out on the soccer field were kids. His confusion only grew when she pulled into a parking space in front of one of the buildings.

Reid pulled into a space by the soccer field and watched as Jane took all of her bags from the car and headed into the building.

This was getting weirder and weirder.

No one went on a romantic picnic at the Austin Animal Shelter.

He sat in his car for a few minutes, trying to make sense of what he'd seen. What was Jane doing?

For that matter, what was *he* doing?

He'd never before given much thought to what his girlfriends did when they weren't with him and he sure as hell had never followed one to find out.

He'd never cared enough.

So why Jane?

What was it about her that made him so crazy?

And what was she doing at the animal shelter?

He had absolutely no answers to the first two questions, and the only answers to the third lay through the doors of the animal shelter.

So he followed Jane.

Through the doors of the building, he found a row of desks on his right and another door straight ahead through which Jane had presumably disappeared. He headed for the door, but was stopped by a woman seated at one of the desks.

"Can I help you?"

Focused on finding Jane, he didn't even glance at the woman. "No, thanks."

Before he made it to the door, the woman practically

leapt over her desk to throw her girth between him and the door. "How can I help you?"

The woman stood before him, arms crossed over her massive chest, peering at him from over the rims of her rhinestone, cat's-eye glasses.

"A woman came through here a few minutes ago. I'm just trying to catch up with her."

The woman's eyes narrowed, her expression suspicious. "Jane?"

Hoping to ease her suspicions, he smiled reassuringly. "Yes, my girlfriend, Jane."

She eyed him up and down, then snorted in apparent disbelief. "*Your* girlfriend?"

Trying to tamp down his growing annoyance, he asked, "Who are you, exactly?"

Her broad shoulders straightened, her chin bumped up. With obvious pride and self-importance, she said, "I approve applications."

"Applications?"

"If you want to adopt a pet, you have to fill out an application first. If I approve your application, then you can visit the animals. Through this door."

"But I don't want to adopt an animal. I just want to see Jane."

"Jane works in the adoption center. If you want to see Jane, you'll have to fill out an application and have it approved."

The words, "You got to be kidding," were on the tip of his tongue, but he bit them back. This woman reminded him so much of the mindless, form-driven bureaucrats who ran the foster-care system. The same ones who'd shuffled him from home to home.

Every rebellious instinct he had roared at him. But

he wasn't the alienated kid he'd once been. He'd learned how to work the system and he knew exactly how to get what he wanted from this kind of woman.

He smiled broadly. "So, if I fill out an application, and you approve it, then I can walk through those doors to the adoption room where Jane works."

"Exactly."

"Then can you get me an application?"

"Applications are by the door."

He grabbed an application, then lowered himself to the chair across from the bureaucrat and began to fill in the requisite information. Name, address, occupation. Still, since he was stuck here, he might be able to get some information from her.

"So, tell me—" he looked for and found the woman's nameplate on her desk "—Glenda, how long have you worked with Jane?"

"I don't work with Jane." Her nose rose a fraction as if she smelled something distasteful. "I'm a full-time employee. Jane is just a volunteer."

"Oh, of course," he said hastily. "I was just wondering if you knew how long she'd worked, I mean, volunteered here."

"Too long." She sniffed to show her lack of interest.

He changed tactics. "I bet you know the ins and outs of this place better than anyone."

Her posture straightened with obvious pride. "As a matter of fact, I do."

He laughed in fake agreement. "I bet you could do any job in this place. If you wanted to."

She nodded, the lines of her face softening to his flattery. "I've often thought that same thing myself. Why, the director of the facility is a total idiot."

He finished one form and started on the next, asking, as subtly as he could, "And the volunteers? How are they?"

"Mostly they just get in the way. Asking questions, taking up my time. Your friend Jane is the worst."

His pen stilled, then he forced himself to keep writing so she wouldn't know she'd piqued his curiosity. "Why is that?"

"You know how pushy she is."

Pushy? Jane?

Well, he supposed she could be pushy—such as last night, when she'd pushed all of his buttons and driven him to make love to her right there on the sofa. Somehow he didn't think that was the kind of pushy Glenda here had been referring to.

"Hmm," he murmured noncommittally.

"Always coming up with some harebrained idea to get more people to adopt pets. She's always wanting the shelter to build playrooms so people can 'bond' with the animals." Her voice dripped with disdain. "Or pipe in music that will make people want to stay longer, like they do at the grocery store. And when the director won't approve it, she and that friend of hers always take it to the city council. You know what Jane's like."

Except he was beginning to think he didn't know what Jane was like at all.

"'Course," the woman rambled on, unprompted, "if they don't approve her proposals, she just does it anyway. Brings her own chairs and music. When it's hot, she even brings drinks to hand to patrons."

Suddenly, the cooler, the chairs, and the backpack made sense.

"She's like a pit bull, that one. Once she's got an

idea, she never lets it go." She must have sensed his growing annoyance, because she hastily added, "Not that it's a bad thing, her wanting to find homes for all those animals. But, geez, she's a little too enthusiastic, if you know what I mean."

In other words, Jane made the paid employees look bad.

He handed over the application without comment, but forced a smile.

Glenda read over the forms, muttering parts aloud to herself. "Reid Forester...own condo...President CEO Forester+Blake ad agency." Her eyes darted to his, clearly impressed. Then her brow wrinkled. "Hey, isn't that where Jane works?"

"Actually, yes."

Glenda laughed as if she'd just gotten the punchline to a joke. "You're her boss, not her boyfriend. I knew it."

"No, actually— Knew what?"

Glenda waved her hand dismissively. "Knew a mousy thing like Jane couldn't attract a man like you."

He kept his opinions firmly to himself while he waited for her to type his information in the computer and stamp "Approved" across his two applications.

But as he finally made it through the two doors that would take him to Jane, he thought about the way the woman had described Jane. Pushy Jane. Mousy Jane. Neither of which bore too much resemblance to the sexy Jane he'd spent the past two nights with.

He couldn't help wondering which Jane he'd find when he walked through those doors.

She didn't see him at first. She stood at the end of a long row of cages, smiling broadly as she talked to a couple. In her arms she cradled a scruffy long-haired white cat. He watched her in absolute fascination. She seemed totally relaxed. Completely at ease.

After a minute she handed the cat over to the couple, scratching the cat under the chin to ease the transition. Then she gestured the couple into the two folding chairs set up along the wall, before pulling a cat brush from her backpack and handing it over, as well.

Just as Glenda had described. The chairs, the music, and Jane, doing everything she could to find a home for the cats.

Something about the scene pulled at his heart. Maybe it was simply seeing her here like this—so at ease, so comfortable, in a way she never was with him. Or maybe it was the simple generosity of her spirit.

He couldn't help thinking of the many caseworkers who'd shuffled him through the system. None of them had shown the passion and commitment Jane showed to these animals. He couldn't help wondering how different his life might have been if even one of them had.

And yet, watching her, he couldn't regret how his life had turned out. Despite his rocky beginning, he'd found a wonderful home with parents who had loved him. He'd found his place, not only in a family, but in the business world, as well.

As he thought of Forester+Blake he felt none of the restrictive panic he usually worked so hard to bury. Advertising might not have even been a profession he'd have chosen on his own, but he was starting to enjoy it, and it had brought him Jane.

In that instant, his relationship with Jane shifted from a business liability—a risk he couldn't resist taking despite his best intentions—to the greatest asset he had.

His relationship with Jane was only a bad idea if it didn't work out. But why wouldn't it work out?

It wasn't as if he was going to fire her. Even if he had to lay off some employees, she'd always have a job—her creative brilliance guaranteed that.

Observing her as she moved from cage to cage to check on the cats, he felt—with deep-in-his-gut certainty—that he could love Jane. That he could spend the rest of his life with her, trying to make her happy.

She cared about these forgotten and abandoned animals. Cared about their quality of life and whether or not they found homes. The care she gave to them and to the people who'd come here showed him more of her beauty than a hundred pieces of revealing lingerie. Her actions here told him more about her passion than a hundred romantic encounters.

Put quite simply, she loved the unlovable. Cared for that which no one else wanted. And if he was very lucky, she might come to care for him, as well.

With the couple settling in with the cat, she finally turned and glanced in his direction. Instantly, she stiffened. Her smile faded and her hand went to smooth her hair.

In that instant he realized Jane was like two separate women. One was gorgeous, sexy, and wild in bed, but she never relaxed, never laughed, never had fun. The other was less of a knockout, but she was relaxed and natural. The relaxed Jane was the one he wanted to have a relationship with. The one he could imagine marrying some day.

The bad news was, he was sleeping with the wrong Jane.

CHAPTER THIRTEEN

"W-WHAT are you doing here?" Jane asked as she crossed the room to where Reid stood.

She fidgeted with the hem of her shirt as she asked the question. As he watched her, it occurred to him that she was nervous enough as it was. If she knew he'd followed her here, it might freak her out.

So he held up his approved application from Glenda. "I came here to adopt a pet."

"You want to adopt a pet?" she asked suspiciously.

"I had Glenda approve my application," he pointed out.

"Glenda?" Jane asked sarcastically. "You're on a f-first-name basis with her?"

"Sure. She was quite talkative."

Jane's eyebrows shot up in disbelief. She shook her head. "In five years, all I've gotten out of her is disapproving grunts. Five minutes with you and you're her bosom buddy."

"She said you volunteer here a lot."

Jane ducked her head, a faint blush moving across her cheek. "I...sure, usually."

A portable CD player sat on one of the cages,

playing the soft tunes of Norah Jones. A nice slow song that would encourage people to linger.

"So that's why you couldn't meet me today?" He moved closer to her, ostensibly to hear her over the music. "Why didn't you say so?"

"One of the reasons. I—" She broke off, her nervousness making her fidgety. She moved a step closer to him and said in a low voice, "I didn't think y-you and I had the kind of relationship where we shared that kind of thing."

Yeah, he didn't think so, either. But he wanted that to change.

However, he was pretty sure she wasn't ready to hear that. So he turned his attention to the cages lining the walls. "So, what kind of cat do you think I should get? Or should I get a dog? I've always thought of myself as more of a dog person."

"You want a dog? Seriously?"

"Sure. Why not?"

"You know, dogs are more work than cats."

"You think I'm afraid of work?" he teased.

A blush crept into her cheeks. "I didn't mean that. But they require more attention. They need to be walked and played with. If you're not at home enough, they get lonely."

"Not a problem."

"But you live in a condo. You don't even have a backyard."

"I live in a great neighborhood to take walks. I walk down to the bakery for breakfast most mornings as it is."

"Down to the bakery?"

Her voice sounded high and nervous. What had he said wrong?

He put his hand on her arm and she turned to face him. "Are you okay? You sound a little tense."

Her gaze flickered to his and then away to the dog kennels. Her words came out in a rush. "Of course I'm okay. Why wouldn't I be okay? I'm great. Here I am, helping you pick out a dog so that you can walk it down to the bakery for breakfast. It's great. Just perfect."

"Jane, you don't—"

"Did you know dogs live up to fifteen years, depending on breed and diet? I looked it up. That's a serious commitment."

She looked so adorably flustered it was all he could do not to pull her into his arms to soothe whatever was bothering her. But he knew where touching her would lead. So far their relationship had been so sexual, he wanted to spend this time with her without having it devolve to that. Even if it killed him.

Still, he couldn't keep himself from stepping closer to her and brushing a stray lock of her hair from her forehead. Once again he smelled the scent of apples on her. This time it didn't have to compete with her expensive perfume. He liked this scent—pure and uncomplicated as it was—better than her perfume.

"I think you might be surprised how much of a commitment guy I am."

Jane's eyes widened slightly. "Reid, I—"

"Excuse me, miss?"

Jane's head jerked in the direction of the two people sitting with the cat.

"We've made up our mind," the man said. The cat sat curled in a contented ball in the woman's lap. "We want to adopt this cat."

"Great. I'll be right there." Jane smiled stiffly, as if

she were equally annoyed with the interruption. To him, she said, "Look around at some of the cats. And don't forget to disinfect y-your hands between cats. You can use the blue stuff from the hand pump on the w-wall or the bottle I brought that's there by the CD players—it smells better."

Before he could say anything else, she was back to helping the couple with the white cat. Unsure how long Jane would be distracted, he played with the tabby kitten for a few minutes before moving on. He picked up the bottle of hand sanitizer she'd left out and squirted a dollop onto his palm. As he rubbed his hands together, he caught a whiff of apples.

He glanced at the bottle. Yep. Country Apple. Another Jane mystery solved.

After setting down the bottle, he peered into the other occupied cat cages. At the far end, a silver and black tabby caught his eye.

As he approached her cage she let out a demanding meow and rubbed her cheek against the door to the cage. Tail in the air, she pranced the length of the cage, showing off her dramatic coloring and spots. She was the most striking cat he'd ever seen. But he'd lived in many foster homes with pets and he knew from a nasty experience with a long-haired Chihuahua that "striking" didn't always mean friendly.

As he bent to read the information card hanging from her cage, her name jumped out at him: Sasha.

The same name Jane had given him that first night on the roof. It couldn't be a coincidence. He glanced at Jane, but she was still busy talking to the couple.

Was this cat special to Jane? Did she feel as if she shared an emotional bond with the cat?

He opened the cage and reached inside to pet Sasha the cat.

For a few seconds, she allowed him to pet her behind the ears but then he tried to stroke her back. As if annoyed that he'd dared to push for more contact, she hissed and swatted at his hand.

He jerked his hand away and slammed the door shut. Okay, she was a bit of a bitch.

As he set the latch, Jane approached from behind him and asked, "What do you think of Sasha?"

Turning towards Jane, he was struck once again by how wholesome she looked dressed in jeans and a T-shirt. So unlike the sex goddess of last night, yet somehow equally appealing.

As he studied her, he realized the delightfully flustered Jane of just a few minutes ago had disappeared. Something in her attitude had shifted. Suddenly she was much more like the person he'd spent last night with.

Unsure what had brought about this change, he measured his words. "She's pretty," he said, then added on—for honesty's sake—"but a little temperamental."

Jane's lips turned down at the corners. Not in a frown, he decided, but in more of a wry smile. "That's the prerogative of a beautiful lady."

As if to reiterate Jane's point, the cat bumped her silvery head against the bars of the cage and purred loudly to attract his attention.

"She's very aggressive," he said.

Jane's gaze dropped and—with just a hint of coyness in her voice—she asked, "You don't like that in a woman?"

Yes, he liked Jane when she was aggressive. But, honestly, he preferred her when she was…human.

Instead of answering, he turned the tables and said, "Tell me about Sasha."

The question seemed to take her aback and her confidence slipped a notch. Jane looked nervously from the cage that housed the gorgeous tabby, to Reid, and then back again. "Well," she began, stumbling for words. "Let's see. Sasha came to the shelter about a month ago. Her case w-worker thought she'd been abused, so she w-was sent to a foster house for—"

"Not the cat. Tell me why you introduced yourself to me as Sasha."

"Oh." She glanced nervously around, as if looking for a distraction, but they were alone now. So she focused all her attention on Sasha's cage. Poking her fingers through the bars, she scratched the cat on the chin. "It's because of my s-s-stutter. I get nervous speaking in front of others and my stutter gets w-worse."

She sounded so embarrassed about it. As if she were revealing some deep, dark secret. Hoping to reassure her, he pointed out, "Speaking in public scares a lot of people. It's the most common phobia in the US."

She chuckled. "Maybe. But with a stutter, it's different. People think you're slow. Or stupid. You saw w-what I was like that day Teresa was called away from the Butler presentation. I couldn't even speak."

He thought back to that day—which now seemed so long ago—and tried to remember the trouble she'd had speaking in front of just him and Matt. People she knew. She'd looked terrified.

How much harder must it have been for her to speak in front of strangers? How much courage must it have taken for her to even volunteer to do the Butler presentation, all on her own?

"And yet when Teresa couldn't do the presentation, you did it for her." Her courage awed him. "You could have talked to me about it, or Matt. We could have had someone else do the presentation."

"And let you think I couldn't do my job? No w-way. Besides, my friend Dorothea convinced me she could help. That by pretending to be someone else, I could overcome my stutter. I know it sounds crazy, but it w-worked."

Actually, it didn't sound crazy at all. He'd heard rumors that a local newscaster used a similar method to overcome his stutter.

"And so you invented Sasha," he mused.

"Yes. Dorothea said to really feel in character I needed a costume. So she fixed my hair. Gave me the blonde highlights. She did my makeup and dressed me in different clothes, things I never w-w-would have worn on my own." Her voice turned wistful. "I almost believed I was someone else. A completely different person. Someone who could do presentations. Someone not afraid to be the center of attention."

Something in her voice reminded him of what she'd said the night before about her parents' divorce. How she'd coped by "slipping under the radar". And now that he thought about it, she was still doing it. She could give the presentation as Sasha because no one would see the real her.

"And that night on the rooftop you ran into me," he mused.

"Yes."

"And I didn't recognize you." All this confusion could have been avoided if only he'd recognized her.

But if he had, would she have had the courage to

offer him half of her dinner? As Jane, would she have eaten with him, flirted with him, and kissed him until he'd nearly lost all control? Maybe not. Maybe he was lucky he hadn't recognized her there in the darkness.

"Why would you recognize me? You didn't even know who I was. I hadn't done anything to pique your interest before then."

Oh, if only she knew how wrong she was.

He laughed, and she snapped around so she could glare at him. "Well, I'm glad this amuses you."

"It doesn't," he said hastily. "Except that...did you honestly think that after working with you for five years, I had no idea who you were?"

"Do you honestly expect me to believe that you did?" She frowned, clearly annoyed by his obtuseness. "In all of those years, you'd never said more than fifteen to twenty words to me. Total."

"Because I knew I made you nervous. Not because I didn't know who you were." He let her consider that for a moment before saying, "Now, about that Sasha thing—"

"I guess that seems ridiculous to you, doesn't it?"

"Actually, no, it doesn't. It was a brilliant and brave solution to your problem. We all get nervous, Jane, feel insecure."

She gave a little snort of laughter. "Most people don't invent alter egos to hide behind, though."

"You're more creative than most people."

"Right."

"You think I always feel confident? I don't. I spend about half my time at work worried I'm making the wrong decisions. That something I've done is going to ruin my father's company."

He glanced up to find her studying him, her forehead puckered into a frown.

"You're a wonderful CEO. I can't believe you'd doubt that."

"You think that because I make you believe it. People need to see the strong CEO, so I act like a strong CEO. It's a persona, just like your Sasha."

"Except that you *are* a wonderful leader."

"As good as my dad?"

Her frown deepened as she considered the question. "Different. He seemed to…I don't know."

"Enjoy it more?" he asked ruefully.

"Maybe." She shot him a cautious look from under her lashes. "I only worked for him for a year, but he seemed more…relaxed. More comfortable."

Before he could ask her what she meant by that, the door to the cathouse opened and a family poured through, the children's energetic laughter ringing off the concrete floor. Definitely a mood killer. Which was probably no worse than he deserved for trying to have a serious conversation at the animal shelter.

Before Jane could slip away from him, he pointed to the cats and asked, "What about you? Which cat do you like?"

She looked a little startled by the question. Her gaze darted to a cage a few down from Sasha's. "Does it matter?"

"I'm just curious." He moved down to the cage Jane had glanced at. Inside sat a bulky gray cat. The cat watched Reid through wide green eyes, but when she caught sight of Jane, she started purring and pawing the air.

"She seems to like you," he pointed out.

Jane sighed, sticking her fingers through the grid so

the cat could nuzzle them. "Yes, Midge and I are old friends. She's been here for months now."

"Really?"

"No one wants to adopt an older cat. People always go for the pretty cats, like Sasha, or the cute young kittens, like Toby there. They overlook cats like Midge. Don't even notice how sweet she is."

Was this more of her keeping her expectations low? Because she thought people would always overlook her?

The thought unsettled him. She was so bright, with her quick wit and her gut-wrenchingly erotic imagination. She had so much to offer, yet she seemed determined to let life pass her by.

He felt a powerful surge of emotion that he could hardly understand, coupled with a sudden need to touch her.

Standing this close to her, he noticed things about her that he'd never noticed before. Without the heavy coverage of makeup, her skin appeared pale to the point of near transparency, almost luminous. He could see the spattering of freckles across the bridge of her nose, the flush that ran across her cheeks and the length of her neck, the faint crinkles at the corners of her eyes and the worry lines between her eyebrows.

But it was her lips that caught and held his attention. Without the coating of red lipstick, her lips were a pale pink, bare even of lip gloss, dry until she skimmed her tongue over them to moisten them. A part of him had always felt weird about kissing a woman wearing lipstick. Glosses were too oily, lipsticks too cakey. Both kept him from enjoying what he really wanted, the taste and sensation of the woman he was kissing. It was like inhaling a woman's perfume when what he wanted was the scent of the woman herself.

But today, Jane wasn't wearing lipstick. If he kissed her, he'd taste only Jane. Pure, unadulterated Jane.

Her gaze softened and he felt her sway towards him. Her lips were soft and moist, the ultimate enticement. His resolve to keep this encounter non-sexual crumbled to dust.

He felt her shiver, and suddenly something that was meant to be purely comforting became more. Heat curled through his body, urging him to pull her even closer. To lower his lips to hers and explore her mouth. She raised her head, ready for his kiss, her lips moist and enticing. Enticing him not just to kiss her, but to mold her body to his, to back her against the wall and take her. To make her his.

"Jane," he murmured, lowering his mouth towards hers.

But before he could kiss her, she jerked away from him. She pulled her arm from his grasp and pressed her lips into a narrow and reproachful line. For a few seconds, she stared at him, her expression clouded and impossible to read. Then she turned to one of the cages and spoke as if nothing had happened.

"This calico here would be ideal for someone away from home a lot. She's sweet-tempered, but very independent. She's..."

Annoyed by her dismissive attitude, he grabbed her arm again and swung her around to face him. "Stop it, Jane."

Her eyes flashed with unsuppressed emotion. "Stop what, Reid?"

"Stop pushing me away."

"I'm not pushing you away."

"All you do is push me away." The firm line of her lips softened and her eyes widened. She was weakening; he could sense it. He raised his hand to her cheek, grazing his fingers against the delicate skin at her temples. "Come on, Jane, give me a break. This is special, and if it's ever going to go—"

She cut him off, averting her face and leaving his hand hanging in midair. "This? What 'this'?"

And just like that, he lost whatever advantage he'd momentarily gained. "This thing between us."

She shook her head emphatically, her ponytail swinging from side to side. "There is no us. There is no this. All this—" she waved her hand back and forth between them, lowering her voice to a whispered hiss that wouldn't be overhead "—was supposed to be just sex. That was the deal, remember? That's what we agreed on."

"I want more," he insisted, jerking her closer to him, wanting to shake some sense into her. Wanting to force her to acknowledge what was happening between them.

"You can't have more." She wrenched away from him and paced to the far end of the room.

And that was when it hit him. Some time in the past few minutes her stutter had disappeared completely.

Suddenly angry, he followed her to the corner and blocked her in. "So that's it, is it, Jane? Or should I call you Sasha?"

She spun around to face him, her eyes wide. "I don't know what you mean."

"Your stutter's gone." She blinked but said nothing, so he pressed further, his total frustration with the situation edging his words. "Here we are in the middle of an important conversation about our relationship, and you're pretending to be someone else."

"Am I? Because as far as I know, you don't have a relationship with Jane. You have one with Sasha."

"That's not fair. Not when you won't let me get close to you." She opened her mouth to protest, but he didn't let her. "You didn't really think I wouldn't notice, did you? How every time we're alone together you try to distract me with sex?"

"Come on, Reid. You can't really expect me to believe that you want to get close to me. Not when you go to such trouble to keep everyone else at a distance."

"You're right. I do keep people at a distance. Especially people at work. I have to do that. I'm the boss. I can't be everybody's best friend and still make the tough decisions when people need to be let go. I can't risk making decisions about the company based on my emotions."

"Well, then," she quipped sarcastically, "you should be thankful that you and I aren't best friends."

"But you're different, Jane. I'm not going to have to fire you. You're too damn good. Surely you can see that."

"All I see is that you don't really know what you want. You may think you want the real Jane, but you don't even know who she is."

When she met his gaze, her eyes were cold and emotionless. The conversation was over and there was nothing he could say to change that.

Jane was wrong. He did want the real her. He just had no idea how to convince her of that. And it made him furious that she wouldn't even let him try.

CHAPTER FOURTEEN

"WE HAVE a problem."

Instead of taking the seat Reid had offered, Jane glanced from him to Matt, trying to quell the sense of disaster in her belly.

This was it. She was going to be fired. At the very least, he was going to pull her from the *Trés Bien* project.

Why else would Reid have asked Matt to sit in on this meeting?

After the whole animal shelter/Sasha debacle, Reid must have decided she was borderline psychotic. And now he undoubtedly didn't want her working on the most important project Forester+Blake had ever tackled. Could she blame him?

Still, after all she'd been through to keep her job, she wasn't about to just walk away now. "Look, I can understand why you might be feeling cautious about having me on the team, but if you'll give me another chance to—"

"This isn't about yesterday," Reid interrupted her. Matt raised his eyebrows in question, but Reid kept talking. "It's about Martin."

"Who?"

"Roger Martin," Matt said. "His team took over the Butler account."

"Oh, right." The guy who thought she was a moron. The Jerk, as she'd taken to calling him.

So, why was *she* here?

"Martin is leaving. He accepted a job with Blume & Blume."

"Blume & Blume, our competitors?" B & B was the biggest agency in town. She didn't wait for Reid or Matt to answer. "So wh-what does this mean? Do Pete and I need to go back to w-working on the Butler account?"

"No," Matt said. "You need to come up with a new pitch for *Trés Bien*."

"What? Y-you're kidding, right?" But the grim expression on Reid's face confirmed he wasn't. "Why would Martin leaving have any effect on the *Trés Bien* ad? He w-wasn't even working on the account. It's not as if we need him..." She trailed off as she saw where this was going.

"He wasn't working on the account," Reid said, "but he did sit in on key meetings."

"You think he'll take our idea to them."

Reid stood, rounded the desk, and propped his hip against the edge. His posture was relaxed, but there was nothing tranquil about the hard glint in his eyes or the tightness in his jaw. Those hinted at the anger simmering beneath his professional façade.

She'd worked with him for five years and had never seen him angry. Now she'd seen it twice in two days. But this time, was he angry at Martin or at her? Or at himself?

"Blume & Blume isn't hiring," he said. "If they took

Martin, it's because he was able to sell them on a great idea for the *Trés Bien* ad."

"But that's illegal. Unethical, at the very best." She protested more out of anger than anything else. In a situation like this, ethics meant very little.

"And if we had more time, maybe we could do something about it. Even if they don't use your original idea, we can't risk it. If we both show up with the same campaign, it'll ruin us. They'll go with another company."

Reid's gaze met hers as he spoke. "We need a new pitch. I need you, Jane. Be brilliant for us."

I need you. Words he'd never said to her outside the bedroom.

The bad news was, he didn't really need her. He needed her ideas. The really bad news was, she was fresh out of ideas.

Jane couldn't get out of there fast enough. Too bad Reid followed her. His pounding footsteps behind her seemed to echo her pounding heart. He caught up with her right outside her cubicle.

"Jane, I know you're upset that we're not going to use the original idea, but—"

She ducked into the cubicle, hoping to defray whatever damage he was doing by chasing her down the hall. Thankfully Pete wasn't at his desk and no one else seemed to be paying them any attention. "That's not why I'm upset."

"Come on, I saw your expression in there. You don't want to give up the elevator idea."

"Of course I don't want to give up my initial idea. It's a good idea. But that's not why I'm upset."

Hoping he'd just leave it at that, she flopped down into her desk chair and wiggled her mouse to turn off her screen saver.

"Look, if I'm going to come up with another idea, I've got to get to work. So, if that's all…"

Reid braced his hand on the back of her chair and turned it to face him. With one hand on the edge of her cubicle wall and the other by her shoulder, he'd effectively trapped her.

The hard edge still hadn't left his eyes. Nothing he'd said during the meeting had indicated he was angry with her, which should be a relief, but wasn't. Something was still eating at him. Something that had made him pull back from her.

Or maybe he was just respecting the boundaries she'd insisted on. She was the one who'd wanted to keep their sexual relationship separate from their working relationship. So why did his chilly attitude now bother her? "Talk to me, Jane. If you're upset, I need to know why. I can't fix it otherwise."

"Are you sure you can fix it at all?"

"What's that supposed to mean?"

Not even sure where to begin, she shook her head in frustration. "Look, I'd love to come up with another great idea for *Trés Bien*. Nothing would make me happier. But I'm just not sure there are any great ideas left in me."

"I don't believe that." Shaking his head, he pulled back from her, straightening as he tucked his hands in his pockets. "I know the way your mind works. You'll come up with something. You always do."

She wanted to hear at least a hint of sensual promise in that compliment, but his tone was all business. However, that didn't stop the heat curling through her belly. Which was damn annoying, since she really wanted to be angry with him for putting her in this position.

She didn't resent having to come up with a new idea—that was all just part of the business. Just part of her job. But she did resent feeling so confused about their relationship. Feeling so off balance.

Things were so much easier back when she had been just Jane.

She sighed and tried to turn her attention back to her computer.

Unfortunately, Reid loomed behind her, still all businessy. "Tell me what resources you need. What I can do to help."

Wanting just to get rid of him so she could sort through her emotions in peace, she said, "I don't need resources. Or help. All I need is time."

And a miracle.

She'd needed a miracle before, when Dorothea had transformed her into Sasha. But this time she needed a miracle even greater than the powers of pressed make-up and push-up bras.

Worse still, the whole company was depending on her this time. She couldn't let them down.

She only wished her heart would stop aching, because if today had proved anything to her, it had proved that, to Reid, she was far more valuable as an employee than she was as a lover.

"Jane took that better than I would have thought," Matt said when Reid finally made it back to his office. Matt was sipping the cup of coffee Audrey had brought for him, sitting in the chair Jane had abandoned. "Do you think she can pull another rabbit out of her hat?"

"I tend to think Jane can do just about anything she chooses. But in less than five days? I don't know. That's pushing it. Even for her."

Matt stretched his legs out in front of him, looking as if he hadn't a care in the world. "Well, if you trust her, I'm sure she'll be fine."

"You're not worried?" Reid wished he could feel even half as relaxed about this disaster as Matt did.

"Not at all."

"Well, I am." And it was all he could do not to shake Matt by his seemingly unburdened shoulders.

"You worry too much."

Then again, the burden of running Forester+Blake didn't fall on Matt's shoulders. And only Reid could bear the burden of making this colossal mistake.

"My dad left this company in my hands. If it fails, it's my fault. That's why I worry about it."

"Your father left you the company because he wanted you to enjoy it. Not because he wanted you to worry about it.

"Well, he didn't leave it to me expecting it to fail, that's for sure."

"*Trés Bien* is one account."

"But it's an account we need."

"If we lose it, we'll find another. Stop being so hard on yourself."

"If we lose the *Trés Bien* account, it's my fault."

Matt—damn him—chuckled. As if this were all just an amusing game. "You always did have an overactive sense of responsibility."

"I'm serious, Matt. If we lose this account, it's my fault."

Matt shrugged and took another sip of his coffee. "Sure, in an abstract sense, it is. You're the CEO. Everything that happens to the company is your responsibility. You're in charge of everything. Et cetera, et cetera, et cetera."

"Not in an abstract sense. In a real sense. Martin—"

"You can't blame yourself for Martin leaving."

"No, but I blame myself for letting him take Jane's idea. He didn't need to be in on the *Trés Bien* meetings."

"You must have felt differently when you invited him," Matt reasoned.

That was just like Matt, to make excuses for him.

As nice as it would be to let Matt's explanation stand, Reid had to tell him the truth.

"The only reason I invited Martin to the meeting was to prove to him that Jane was capable of handling the *Trés Bien* pitch. He'd made disparaging remarks about Jane…said she was an idiot. It irritated me. I wanted to prove him wrong. I wanted to rub his nose in it."

Matt studied him over the rim of his coffee cup, then slowly lowered the mug to the arm of the chair. "You were angry that he doubted your choice. That he was undermining your leadership."

Reid could do nothing but straighten his shoulders and be brutally honest. "No. I was angry that he doubted Jane. I was feeling protective of her."

Reid watched Matt closely, waiting for his reaction. He forced himself not to look away as understanding dawned in Matt's eyes.

"So, Jane is your mystery woman, after all."

"Yes."

"You lied to me?"

"Not exactly." He crossed to the bookshelf and grabbed a stack of beanbags. As he shuffled the bags from hand to hand, he said, "The last time you and I talked about it, there was nothing going on between Jane and I."

"But now there is," Matt surmised. "Even though you thought it would be a horrible mistake to get involved with an employee."

"Yes."

Matt leaned forward in his chair, steepling his fingers and peering at Reid from over them. "Then she must really mean a lot to you."

For an instant, Matt's words stopped him. Did Jane mean a lot to him?

But he shoved aside the question before he could even begin to formulate an answer. "What matters," he said to Matt, "is that I've compromised a major project because I got too involved with an employee. If I'd just kept my distance, this never would have happened."

Matt shook his head, meeting his gaze with far more understanding than Reid could offer himself. "It's pointless to think that way." He leaned forward, bracing his elbows on his knees. "I've watched you these past couple of weeks. You've enjoyed yourself more at work than you ever have in the past. Now that I know about Jane, I understand why. If getting involved with her caused you to make one bad decision, it's worth it if you're no longer miserable at work."

Which was all well and good for Matt to say.

Reid couldn't be as easy on himself. Unable to sit still any longer, he paced to the bank of windows and stared out of them. "You don't understand. Ever since I took over the company, this is exactly the situation I've been most afraid of."

"That you'd date an employee and lose an account over it?" Matt asked glibly. "That seems a bit far-fetched."

Reid sucked in a deep breath, determined not to take his frustration out on Matt, no matter how annoying he was being. "No, I've been afraid of getting too involved with my employees. Afraid that if I did I wouldn't be able to make the tough decisions, that I wouldn't be able to fire people when we lost accounts."

He turned around to meet Matt's gaze. "I thought I was safe with Jane. I thought because she was so good I'd never be in a position where I might have to fire her. It just never occurred to me that she'd still affect my ability to make good decisions. And now I've screwed up everything."

Matt stood and crossed to his side. He clapped his hand on Reid's shoulder and met his gaze. For once, there was no merry twinkle in his eyes, no easy acceptance. Just the same affection his gaze had always held, mixed with concern.

"For once, forget about the company. Business will sort itself out. It always does. Just think about how you feel and what you want. It's obvious you care deeply about Jane. Maybe you've even fallen in love with her."

Reid opened his mouth to protest, but immediately snapped it shut. Was he in love with Jane?

He just didn't know. He'd never been in love. Never even felt love until he was well into his teens. What basis did he have for comparison?

Luckily, Matt didn't wait for him to respond. "If you want this to work, you can make it work. The company doesn't have to have anything to do with it. And if you think it does, then you have to ask yourself, are you really afraid of hurting the company, or are you afraid of something else?"

Before Reid could ask Matt what he meant by that cryptic question, Matt turned and left, quietly shutting the door behind him. Leaving Reid alone with his thoughts. Alone with a probing question that Reid didn't even want to ask.

CHAPTER FIFTEEN

MATT'S WORDS HAUNTED REID for the rest of the day.

Yes, he was afraid of hurting the company. The financial security of Forester+Blake had been his first concern ever since his father had died five years ago.

But was there more to his devotion to Forester +Blake than just that? Was Matt right?

The question nagged at him, preventing him from accomplishing any work at all. He wanted to see Jane. To talk this all through with her. But he knew that was impossible. She was stuck back in her cubicle, hard at work on the *Trés Bien* ad.

The ad she had to redo because of his screwup. Under the circumstances, he could hardly burden her further with his personal problems.

So he forced himself to stay locked away in his office until well after five, staring blankly at financial reports without seeing them. Finally, his resolve cracked and he went in search of her.

She wasn't at her desk, which surprised him, because she usually worked until at least six. He checked the surrounding cubicles, the break room, and even the conference room. She didn't even answer her cell phone.

As he took the elevator down to the lobby, he was mentally making a list of all the places around town she might be, when it hit him. Instead of heading for his car, he took the elevator up to the top floor, and then the stairs to the roof.

Sure enough, there she was, leaning against the edge of the wrought-iron table, her hands braced on either side of her hips, her voluptuous shape silhouetted against the sun as she stared out at the view of downtown.

For a moment he simply watched her, allowing his heart to flood with tenderness. There was a twinge of fear there, as well.

He had so much riding on the slim shoulders of this complex and crazy woman. Not just the *Trés Bien* ad, but so much more. His personal happiness. And—he was beginning to think—his future, as well.

In some ways, he barely knew her. She fought so hard to keep him out. But in other ways, he knew all he needed to know. She was smart and witty, once she opened up. Self-deprecating. Caring. Devoted to what she believed in. Most of all, she made him happy. And just watching her brought him a kind of peace he hadn't felt in years.

As he made his way across the roof to her side, he told himself it would be enough. Now if only he could convince her.

When he was a few feet away, she spun around to face him.

"I'm glad I didn't miss the sunset," he said.

From this distance, in this light, he couldn't read her expression. After a moment, she turned back to the view without saying anything.

He went to stand by her side, but the view didn't hold his attention. Looking at her, he couldn't help but think of the last time they'd been up here, just a few short weeks ago.

Staring down at her, he mused, "How in the world did I not recognize you that night?"

She slanted a look in his direction. "It was dark." Turning back to the view, she wrapped her arms around her chest. "Besides, people see what they want to see."

"I suppose you're right. I knew I was attracted to you, but I thought I couldn't act on it. So when I saw you that night up here on the rooftop, I saw a stranger. Someone I could be attracted to. Someone I could get involved with without having it mess up my life or complicate matters."

She stiffened. "Sorry I messed up your plan."

He reached for her just as she was pulling away from him. Wrapping his hands around her upper arms, he pulled her closer, making her look up at him. "I'm not sorry. Being with you has made me realize just how empty my life has been."

Now that she was facing him, he could see her features more clearly. Half of her face was illuminated by the fading sunlight, half was cast in shadow. She was like that—even after all the time they'd spent together, she was still a bit of a mystery.

He studied her, waiting for some reaction to his words, but she had none, so he pressed on, needing her to understand what he'd only recently begun to understand about himself.

"I never wanted to be an adman. It wasn't something I'd have picked for myself."

"But it's your father's company, so you do it for him."

He nodded. "But I've never resented it. I loved my

parents. They took me in, gave me a home and family. Things I never dreamed of having for myself. I guess even now that they're gone, I just want to make them proud."

With her head bobbed slightly to the side, she studied him. "He w-would be proud. He loved you very much, even before y-you came home to run the company. But if it doesn't make you happy—"

"That's just it. I always felt like I owed everything to the company. I was okay giving everything to the company. I was okay with the fact that it never made me happy. But now…"

He broke off, dropping his hands from her arms. Damn, this was harder than he'd thought it would be.

Shoving his hands into his pockets, he paced to the edge of the rooftop and stared out at the city below.

"But now…" she prodded from behind him.

"But now I realize the company was just an excuse. Just a reason to keep people at a distance." He forced himself to turn back and face her. "It's hard for me to let people get close. I don't know, maybe it's hard for anyone without a family. You go from foster home to foster home. From school to school. It's easiest to just keep your distance from everyone, then you don't miss them when you move on.

"I didn't realize until today that I was still doing it. Still keeping everyone at arm's length. My parents were the last people—hell, maybe the only people—I was really close to. But you, Jane…you snuck right past my defenses."

He thought he saw her eyes widen—thought he saw a flash of emotion in her eyes—but in fading light he could hardly tell for sure.

"What are you saying, Reid?"

"I've fallen in love with you. I know this complicates things at work. I know this isn't what we agreed upon, but—"

Before he could even finish his sentence, she was in his arms. Pressing her body to his, she wrapped her arms around his neck and pulled his mouth down to hers.

Part of him wanted to resist, to finish what he'd been about to say. But he'd never been able to resist her. Not that first night, when he'd thought she was just Sasha. Not when he'd realized she was Jane. And certainly not now, when he'd realized she was the woman he loved.

Her mouth was hot under his. There was nothing timid in her kiss, only fierce passion. Relentless and demanding. He felt his body quickening in response. Felt his very soul calling out to hers.

Passion hit him on a surge of emotion. The powerful need not just to have sex with her, but to mate with her. To make her his. Totally and completely his.

She must have felt a similar calling, because her hands grasped frantically at his chest, shoving his jacket off his shoulders as she arched against him.

Groaning his name, she fingered the buttons of his shirt impatiently.

Only then did he realize that she'd never responded to his declaration, but by then he was too far gone. Too drawn in by her passion.

Her heated response had to mean she felt the same way.

She hadn't said she loved him, too, only because she felt it didn't need to be said.

Once he made her his, everything else would sort itself out. Everything would be okay.

Everything was not okay. Not by a long shot.

Unfortunately, he didn't realize that until the next morning.

This time, at least, he woke up with her still in his arms. Sleepy and mussed, she looked adorable. And delightfully sexy. And he would have loved to have spent the morning making love to her...if only she'd said she loved him, too.

Or, at the very least, even hinted at some deeper emotion. He knew she felt more than she was letting on. Knew she was hiding her emotions from him—and maybe from herself, as well.

He didn't need a declaration of love from her. Just some hint that she at least acknowledged what was happening between them.

Unfortunately, all he'd gotten from her was sex. Fabulous sex, yes. But only sex.

As he leaned over her in bed and brushed her hair from her eyes, he decided to give her one last chance. "Morning, gorgeous," he murmured. Nuzzling the side of her neck, he added, "Man, I love waking up to you." Then he laughed and nibbled at her ear. "Actually, I just love you."

Jane stilled as his words sank in. The power of his words shoved aside even the delightful sensation of his mouth on her neck and ear.

Something clenched around her heart, making it difficult for her to breathe. She squeezed her eyes closed, bracing herself against his onslaught. She'd managed to keep him at bay all last night, so why was it so much harder this morning? Why did she feel so much more vulnerable to him now?

She prayed he would keep kissing her. Prayed he wouldn't notice the silence gaping between them.

But he did notice, and, when she didn't respond, he pulled back to stare down at her. "You're not going to say anything, are you?"

Frankly, she didn't know what to say. So she bit down on her lip and held her silence.

With a groan of frustration he rolled off her to the edge of the bed and stood. "So that's it, is it? I tell you I love you and you say nothing. Again."

She sat up, clutching the edge of the sheet to her chest. "I don't know what you want me to say."

"How about, 'I love you, too'? That's the standard response. Or even, 'I love waking up with you' would do. Not perfect, but a step in the right direction. Hell, even, 'Thanks, Reid, that's nice to know' would be better than nothing."

Shaking her head, she swung her legs over the side of the bed and grabbed her robe from the back of the chair. "I'm sorry I can't say any of those things…it's just…"

He rounded the bed and grabbed her forearm, forcing her to look up at him. "Just what?"

Pulling her arm from his grasp, she backed away from him. "Nothing's changed. It's still just sex."

He reached for her, but she stayed firmly just beyond grasp. "This isn't just sex. Not for either of us. I really care about you."

"You don't care about me." Her voice rose sharply as she spoke. "You don't even know me."

He closed the distance between them. "Of course I know you."

She hated the twinge of panic she heard in her voice. She continued to back away. "Oh, you may think you know me, but you don't know the real me."

"I do know you," he said with a fierceness that tore at her. "I don't know everything about you, but no one does at the start of a relationship. And I can't think of anything I want to do more than get to know the rest of you."

Oh, how she wanted to believe that. She wanted it so badly, she almost gave in to him completely. Instead, she struggled to regain control of the conversation. "I can think of several things you've enjoyed more than getting to know me." She slinked over to his side and pressed herself against him. "Most of them we did just last night."

He cupped her bottom through the layers of terry cloth and pulled her against him. Her lips parted, waiting for his kiss.

Even now, her blood throbbed in her veins, silently urging him to kiss her, to toss aside her robe along with this ridiculous conversation that would only cause her more pain.

But before she could seal the deal, he stepped away from her. "It's not going to work this time."

Her eyes fluttered open. "What's not going to work?"

"Distracting me with sex. You do it all the time."

She quickly averted her eyes. "I don't know what you mean." She tilted her head so a curtain of hair shielded her face from him.

"Sure you do." As if unwilling to let her get away with even that, he tucked a lock of hair behind her ear. "You complain that I don't know the real you, but every time I start to get close to you, you distract me with sex."

"That's not true," she protested.

"Isn't it? What were you doing just now? What about last night on the roof? Or Saturday night at my apartment?"

"I—" She wrapped her arms around her chest defensively. "I don't know what you're talking about."

"So you keep saying." He closed the distance between them and tugged at her hands, carefully untying the knot she'd made with her arms. "Why are you so afraid to let me in?"

She resisted him, tensing her arms and keeping her barriers firmly in place. "Why are you so sure you want in?"

"Isn't it obvious? I'm in love with you."

That again. She didn't want to have this conversation, but he just wouldn't let it go. "That's ridiculous."

"Why?"

She snatched her hands back from his. "Because you don't know me. You're attracted to this person you think I am. This person who's sexy and confident. Who can give presentations and write ads for *Trés Bien*. But that person isn't real. She doesn't exist."

She gestured emphatically as she spoke, her emotions were so close to the surface. Emotions she didn't want him to see.

He tried to pull her into his arms as if to comfort her. "She looks pretty real to me."

But she didn't let him touch her. "This relationship is an illusion. There's nothing to it but sex." She slowed her speech, enunciating each word as if she were talking to a child. "The woman you think you're falling in love with isn't real."

He studied her for a long moment, and she was sure he'd see what she meant. Wrapped in her armor-like robe, with her hair disheveled and her complexion mottled by her heightened emotions, she was a far cry from the sexy, sophisticated woman he'd "met" that first night on the Prescott's roof. She looked neither glamorous nor refined.

She waited for him to see her as she really was, but he just continued gazing at her with love in his eyes.

Which only drove home that she'd let this go on far too long. "I'm not Sasha. There's nothing of her in me. Nothing. Sasha is beautiful and confident and sexy. And I'm none of those things."

"But you are," he insisted.

"No, Reid. You want to believe I am. You've totally bought into this fantasy you have of me as the perfect woman for you." She started pacing nervously. "I'm supposed to be not just beautiful and sexy, but I'm supposed to be clever, too. I'm supposed to be the one who comes up with the great idea that's going to save the company, but I gotta tell you…so far that's not happened. I've been working my butt off here and I have no new clever, sexy ideas for the pitch."

It took him a moment to catch up with her train of thought. "Is that what's bothering you? You're afraid you won't come up with an idea for the ad campaign?"

"Among a great deal of other things, yes."

"What are you saying, Jane? That you can't be my girlfriend and do the ad campaign?"

"Yes. No…I don't know, maybe."

"You want me to choose between you and the company?" he asked incredulously. "Because I—"

"No!" Her voice rang with shock, but then she sighed. "I don't want you to choose. This is your father's company. You love it. You said over and over again that it's the most important thing in your life. I'd never make you choose. And I'd never do that to the company." Her shoulders stiffened as indignation set in. "I care about Forester+Blake, too. I care about the people who work here. Just how selfish do you think I am?" But then she shook her head. "Don't answer that. It's irrelevant, since you don't know who I really am, anyway."

He grabbed her by the shoulders and gently shook her. "Stop saying that. I know you, Jane." She opened her mouth to protest, but this time he didn't let her finish. "I don't care what you look like; that's not the point. I know who you are inside. That's the woman I'm falling in love with. The woman who's smart and funny, even though she's shy. The woman with the wicked imagination and quick sense of humor. I don't care what you're wearing or how you do your hair. It's you I want."

As he spoke, her eyes searched his face, slowly widening as his words sank in.

"You've spent your whole life slipping under people's radar, Jane Demeo, and you almost slipped under mine, but you didn't. And I'm not going to let you go."

Shaking her head, she whispered, "I'm sorry, Reid. I don't see how I can ever live up to this fantasy you have of me."

"I'm not in love with the fantasy. I'm in love with you." But she didn't respond. So he stepped back and folded his arms across his chest. "Are you even going to try to make this work?"

"I'm sorry. But I know, sooner or later, you'll realize what I mean. Eventually, I'll disappoint you."

"You won't," he insisted. But then he rocked back on his heels, understanding slowly dawning in his eyes. "But that's not what you're really worried about, is it? You're not just worried about disappointing me sooner or later. You're worried I'll disappoint you."

"No." But her protests sounded weak.

She propped her hips against the edge of the sink, as if the fight had taken everything out of her and she no longer had the energy to stand. "We had a few really great weeks. Shouldn't that be enough?"

"I want more." He crouched before her, grasping her shoulders, and forcing her to look him in the eye. "You think this is easy for me? I've been pushing people away my whole life, too. It just seemed easier that way. But now I want more. I can't promise I'll never disappoint you, but I can promise that I'm not going to desert you."

"That's not—"

But he didn't bother fighting with her over it and instead plowed ahead with his argument. "Yes, these past few weeks have been great. Yes, the fantasy has been nice. But now I want the real thing. I want a real relationship. I don't care if it's not perfect. I'd rather have reality than fantasy. I think it's worth the risk. Do you?"

CHAPTER SIXTEEN

WEEK from hell didn't even begin to describe it. Between working frantically on new ideas for the *Trés Bien* campaign—all of which sucked—and trying desperately to avoid Reid and convince him she needed time, by the time Thursday rolled around, Jane was physically and emotionally exhausted.

And she still had no answers for Reid.

She wanted to believe him. She wanted to take the risk, but part of her knew he didn't really see her as she was. He only saw what he wanted to see.

And despite his reassurances that she was enough just as she was, she couldn't shake the fear that one day soon he'd realize what a fraud she was. She was already way too emotionally involved with him. Did she dare get in even deeper, knowing it could lead to heartache as she'd never known? Did she dare be that brave?

For the first time in the five years she'd been volunteering at the animal shelter, she actually considered calling Dorothea to cancel.

In the end, she'd made it down to the animal shelter only because it was a surefire way to avoid Reid.

Besides, staying at home to stare at a blank notepad wasn't helping much.

She walked into the cathouse to find Dorothea trying to "sell" Sasha to a single mom and her teenage boys.

"We were really hoping for a long-haired kitten," Jane heard the mother say.

Ten minutes later, when they left empty-handed, Jane asked, "So what's the deal? I thought Sasha had a waiting list. Shouldn't she be gone by now?"

Dorothea sighed, running her perfectly sculpted nails across the fringe of her bangs. "The first two families on the waiting list brought her back within twenty-four hours. They claimed she was unfriendly."

Jane had to bite back a laugh. "Well, we could have told them that." Then she glanced at Sasha's cage and felt suddenly a little sad for the cat. She stuck her fingers through the bars of the cage and Sasha bumped her forehead against them. "Tough break, old girl." Sasha purred, turning her head so Jane could scratch her ear. To Dorothea, Jane said, "She can be rather sweet, you know. She just likes to dole out her affection on her own terms."

"Hmm." Dorothea seemed to be studying the cat. "I'm not sure I blame her. Because she's pretty, she gets more attention than the other cats. But that means more strangers petting her and touching her. More little kids poking their fingers into her cage. It must be hard always being the center of attention."

"Tell me about it," Jane said under her breath.

But not softly enough, because Dorothea turned her inquisitive gaze on Jane. "I've been wondering how your little project has been coming along."

"Just great." Jane pulled her fingers from Sasha's cage and began unloading her backpack.

Hand sanitizer, cat toys, and CDs all made it to their respective spots, but when she slammed the CD player down a little harder than she meant to she forced herself to take a deep breath and try to calm down.

"You want to tell me what's bothering you?" Dorothea asked in that calming maternal voice of hers.

"I—" Jane popped open her folding chair and sank into it. "I don't know wh-what's bothering me."

But that wasn't really true. She knew exactly what was bothering her.

All of her life, she'd wanted to be someone like Sasha. Someone cool and collected. Someone sexy and in control. Someone who could just open her mouth and words would come pouring out. All the right words, with just the right tone and inflection. With no awkward, embarrassing stutter.

She'd dreamed of it all her life, and now, finally, when her dream came true, it wasn't anything like she'd thought it would be.

"I guess I just… Being Sasha wasn't like wh-what I thought it would be."

"Hmm," Dorothea murmured. "Being someone else never is."

"I thought it would make everything easier, but instead it made everything harder. It complicated work and it completely mucked up my personal life."

As briefly as she could, she explained about Reid. And about his mistaken impression that he was in love with her.

"I see," Dorothea said. "And how do you feel about him?"

She sank her head into her palms and finally admitted aloud, "I think I'm falling in love with him."

Dorothea's expression brightened. "Well, that's

just—" then she noticed the bleak look Jane sent her "—wonderful," Dorothea finished lamely.

"No, it's not wonderful."

"So I gather." Dorothea pursed her lips. "Why exactly isn't it wonderful that the man you think you love loves you in return?"

"Oh, he thinks Sasha is great. Can't keep his hands off of her."

"I'm not sure I follow."

Jane stood. "He thinks he's falling in love with Sasha. But I'm not Sasha, I'm Jane. And I'm tired of being Sasha."

"I think I'm confused."

"You're not the only one."

"You told me," Dorothea pointed out, "that he recognized you as Jane."

"He did. I mean, he does. He knows I'm Jane. But he doesn't know the real Jane. The whole time we've been dating, I've acted like Sasha. Confident and sexy."

"So?"

"So that's the w-woman he thinks he's falling in love with. That's the woman he thinks I am. But that's not the real me. That's just an illusion. And I'm tired of maintaining it."

"Have you talked about this with your friend Keegan?"

"Yes." And for once his advice had been good, if not particularly helpful.

"And what did he have to say about it?"

"He said I deserved to be with someone who loved me as I really am."

Dorothea nodded. "That's good advice."

"Or, it would be if I knew who that was."

A new cat in a nearby cage pawed at her through the

bars of its door, so she absently rubbed its forehead as she spoke. "I don't w-want to be in a relationship where I have to work this hard. I want to be able to relax and just be myself. And Reid accused me of being afraid of taking risks. He said I was afraid the reality wouldn't live up to the fantasy."

Dorothea studied her for a moment. "Let me ask you something. What exactly do you mean by 'be your-self'? Is this—" she gestured to Jane "—who you think you really are?"

"That's just it. I'm not sure I know anymore."

"Then how can you be sure he isn't in love with the woman you are?"

Dorothea rested her hands on Jane's shoulders. "So you admit that the real you is neither Sasha nor Plain Jane Demeo, but rather someone in between?"

Jane begrudgingly nodded. "I'll admit I look differ-ent, but that doesn't mean I am. Hair gel and a good foundation don't make me a better person."

"I never said different was better. Besides, they may not make you a different person, but they are signs of how much you've grown. You've always been afraid of being the center of attention. You've hidden behind bulky clothes and a nondescript hairstyle because you wanted people to ignore you. You've hidden behind your stutter, too."

Jane frowned, more than a little unnerved by how accurate that sounded. "So?"

"So, clearly you no longer need to hide behind those things. Today when you walked in, I saw a confident, beautiful woman who's comfortable with who she is." Dorothea's smile broadened. "Have you considered the possibility that your Mr. Forester really is in love with the woman you've become?"

Dorothea's words haunted Jane long into the night. She lay awake, staring at the ceiling, remembering the conversation. It was a nice fantasy, imagining she could be herself and have the guy of her dreams.

A little too nice for Jane to ever really believe it was possible. Reid had been the stuff of fantasies for too long.

And yet…her fantasies weren't really about Reid the man. They were about Reid the illusion. The man she'd imagined him being, not the man he really was.

In many ways, the man she'd been fantasizing about was no more real than her Sasha. He was the dashing, handsome businessman. Reid was all those things, but he was so much more, as well. He was funny and thoughtful. Lonely, now that his family was gone. And maybe even a little lost sometimes.

He had depths she'd never imagined in her sexual fantasies. As much as she'd tried to keep a handle on her emotions, she still very much wanted to explore all those parts of him she'd never imagined he had.

She didn't want to give up on the fantasy of being in love with Reid. She wanted the fantasy to be reality. But would it work?

Somehow, in the past few weeks, everything in her life had gotten helplessly out of whack. As a result, her psyche was a muddled mess. It was as if she needed feng shui for her emotions.

She needed to find balance. Balance between her personal life and her professional life. Balance between Sasha and Jane. Balance between her creativity and her passion.

That thought sent her bolt upright in bed. For a moment, she stared into the darkness, listening to the hum of her air conditioner, watching the shadows of the trees outside her bedroom window, waiting for the images flashing through her mind to coalesce. When they did, she flipped on her lamp and reached for the notepad.

CHAPTER SEVENTEEN

SHE HAD asked for time, so Reid tried to give it to her.

He hadn't called her at home. Hadn't gone by the animal shelter. Hadn't even skulked around her desk at work. But devoting so much time and energy into staying away from Jane was slowly driving him crazy.

It frustrated the hell out of him knowing her team was trying to throw together a kickass ad for *Trés Bien* and there was nothing he could do to help. But it was ten times more frustrating knowing she was out there deciding the fate of their relationship.

Jane held his entire life—both work and personal—in her delicate little hands. And there wasn't a damn thing he could do about it. Except trust that her brilliance would pull the company through, and hope that she'd trust him enough to let him into her heart.

Still, the waiting was just about killing him.

Which was why he was so relieved to see her at his office door early Friday morning. She knocked on the door frame just before eight.

His heart tightened at the sight of her. She was dressed simply, in jeans and a knit shirt. The outfit emphasized her long legs and her generous curves. Her hair fell in layers around her face, it, too, simple and subdued. There was nothing plain or frumpy about her, nothing vamped up or oversexed. She was neither Plain Jane Demeo nor Sasha, but the woman he'd known all along she was inside.

As she crossed his office, he stood, rounding the corner of the desk to meet her halfway. He wanted nothing more than to pull her into his arms and kiss her. The three days that had passed since he'd last held her had been too long.

But before he reached her, she held out a black portfolio.

He looked at it, then back at her, for an instant forgetting the ad she'd been working on.

She pushed the portfolio into his hands. "The *Trés Bien* ad."

Finally, he took it from her. As he reached for the latch, she stopped him.

"It's good." She bumped up her chin and met his gaze fully, as if daring him to argue with her.

He felt a surge of pride. Just a few weeks ago, he'd practically had to shove bamboo shoots under her fingernails to get her to admit her work was good.

"I'm sure it is." He tossed the portfolio onto his desk. "What about us?"

She didn't meet his gaze, but shoved her hands into her back pockets and seemed to be studying his shoes. "Just look at the ad."

Then, with a sigh, he unzipped the portfolio and flipped it open. Like her ad for Butler, the drawings were just rough sketches done in pencil.

The first was of a woman dressed in lingerie. The drawing showed her standing before a mirror, her hands at her hair as if she were styling it. Her robe draped off her shoulder to reveal a bra strap and parted at her legs to show off garters and stockings. On her feet she wore high-heeled slippers, the kind with feathers across the top. The tagline read: "Sure, it's great to be a Sex Goddess."

He chuckled. Even with the cartoon sketches, the woman in the fancy lingerie was the classic image of the *Trés Bien* model. He was instantly intrigued and couldn't wait to see where Jane was going with this, so he flipped the page.

This sketch showed the same woman walking across a bedroom towards a ringing telephone. At the edge of the shot, a cat was just running into the picture, and a dog was barking "off screen". This time the tagline read: "But life's hectic."

In the next shot, the dog chases the cat in front of the woman and she trips on her high-heeled shoes. In the next, she's sitting on the floor, her elaborate hair-style has fallen down, her robe is coming open, and the cat is playing with the feathers on her shoes. "Seri-ously? Who has time to be a Sex Goddess?"

In the final two shots the woman was dressed in jeans and vee-necked T-shirt—not unlike the outfit Jane wore this morning. The woman's curls were pulled into a simple ponytail and her feet were bare as she opened the front door to a tall, handsome man. In the last picture, the pair was back in her bedroom, where he pulled off her T-shirt to reveal a *Trés Bien* bra.

"Wouldn't you rather be yourself? With maybe just a little Sex Goddess thrown in?"

Reid laughed as he set the portfolio aside. The ad was great. Pure Jane. Funny and sexy, with just a little bit of bite.

And a whole lot of herself.

Whether she meant the ad to be a message to him or not, he'd certainly gotten her point. It was what she'd been telling him. She didn't want to be just a sex goddess. She wanted to be herself. And she wanted him to want her for who she was.

Didn't she realize he already did?

Apparently not. She was so hung up on the idea that he wanted her just for sex or just for the work she did.

But why couldn't she see that who she was was deeply enmeshed in the work she did? It would be impossible for him to love her without valuing her work.

He looked up to find her studying him. He flipped the portfolio closed and tossed it onto his desk.

"You're right," he said. "It's good." She nodded, the smile on her face undeniably proud. It brightened her whole face. Practically made her glow. "Will you come to New York with me to pitch it to *Trés Bien*?"

It wasn't the question he really wanted to ask, but still he held his breath, waiting for her answer.

"No. I spoke with Teresa yesterday. She'll be back at work this afternoon. She should do the pitch. She's the best and you need the best for this."

"I need you." He stretched his hand out to her, all but pleading her to come.

To his surprise, she stepped forward and placed her hand in his. As she spoke, she looked at him from under her lashes, coyly gauging his reaction. "It's just that I don't want to leave the cats alone. Not so soon after bringing them to a new home."

"The cats?"

"Sasha and Midge. I'm picking them up this afternoon. It's part of my new plan to take more risks."

Hope rose within him, but he needed to be sure. "Your new plan?"

"I decided you were right." She spoke haltingly, as if unsure of how he would receive her words. "I've been dreaming too long. I need to start living. Trade in the fantasy for reality."

He closed his eyes in relief and sank to the edge of his desk. With a gentle tug on her hand, she stepped between his legs. His hands settled easily onto her generous hips and he gritted his teeth against the need to hug her tightly to his chest. His relief was too new and he didn't want to crush it. "Any chance I fit into this new plan?"

She, however, had no compunction about plastering her body to his. Her head sank to his shoulder even as he felt her nodding. "Actually, you do. I thought maybe, when you got back, we could go pick out a puppy together."

He froze. "A puppy?"

"Yeah, a puppy. A nice medium-sized breed that we can enjoy for a long time."

"A puppy," he repeated. He nudged her away so he could study her expression. "You know, I was kinda hoping for a declaration of love here. You know, to match the one I gave you."

The smile she gave him was bright and hopeful. "I do love you, Reid." Then, almost as if she couldn't resist, she added, "You know, dogs live up to fifteen years. That's a big commitment."

He couldn't help laughing at her logic. And wondering if this wonderful, crazy woman would ever make sense to him. Or if it even mattered.

"Is that how long you want us to be together?"

"No, of course not. I want us to be together forever.

I'm ready to trade in the fantasy of unrequited love to the reality of love that's...well, requited."

He pulled her back to him, lowering his mouth to hers and showing her, the only way he knew how, exactly how much her love was requited.

EPILOGUE

JANE woke with the sun in her eyes and a wet dog nose pressed against the back of her neck. Mostly, it was the dog nose that brought her to full alertness.

She jerked upright and scrambled out of bed. "Trey, that's gross." Glaring at him, she rubbed the dog off the back of her neck. "You know you're not allowed in the bed."

Trey—a pudgy beagle mix—lay across Reid's side of the bed with his paws neatly tucked under his body. At her chastisement, he seemed to frown. He dropped his chin to his front paws and looked up at her with an expression of bewildered remorse. He didn't know what he'd done wrong, but he was very, very sorry.

Just as his sorrowful expression was beginning to melt her heart, she noticed the thick satin ribbon tied around his neck.

What in the world…?

She reached across the bed to tug on the red tail-end of the bow. The knot slipped loose and the ribbon—weighted down to a white envelope—fell away from his neck.

Jane pulled out the simple note card. "What has he done now?"

But Trey merely stared back at her.

As she held the card, she couldn't help thinking of the countless fantasies she used to harbor that all started with Reid sending a note to her desk at work.

In a thousand years, she never would have dreamed Reid would one day be sending a note to her bed. Via their dog, no less.

Three months had passed since they'd won the *Trés Bien* account and picked out Trey the dog to celebrate the occasion. Trey was an exceptionally good dog—sweet-natured, well behaved and very patient with the cats, letting Sasha boss him around mercilessly, even though she was a good eight pounds lighter than he was.

Shaking her head at how much her life had changed, she unfolded the note and read the message inside. Scrawled in Reid's masculine handwriting were the words, "Why not walk Trey down for breakfast at Sweetish Hill? I'll meet you there."

She looked back at Trey. "Did you put him up to this?"

Trey merely thumped his tail against the bed.

She dressed quickly, unsure how long Reid had been waiting or how late she'd slept. Luckily the walk down to Sweetish Hill went quickly, with Trey hurrying along beside her, as eager to see Reid as she was.

She found Reid sitting at their favorite table, a newspaper spread out in front of him, an empty coffee mug by his hand, as if he'd been calmly waiting for her for hours.

He stood when she approached. Taking Trey's leash from her hands, he pulled her into his arms and kissed her soundly.

"Been w-waiting long?" she asked when he finally let her up for air.

"My whole life."

Now, especially around Reid, Jane no longer needed the disguise of Sasha. Her stutter was still as much a part of her as it had always been. But it no longer made her uncomfortable. She knew he loved her just as she was.

He looped Trey's leash around the back of his chair and then held out the other chair for her. Only then did she notice the plate waiting at her spot at the table. On it sat a chocolate croissant, and, beside that, a small black velvet ring box.

Her gaze darted to Reid's. "What is this?"

Instead of waiting for him to answer, she reached for the box. Before she could open it, he wrapped her hands in his so that together they cradled the box.

"I know this is soon," he began. "And I know you probably want to wait. But I know already you're the woman I want to spend the rest of my life with."

With her heart pounding and her eyes prickling with tears, she nodded. "It's not too soon. I know it, too."

And with that, she launched herself into his arms.

This was one time when reality was definitely better than her fantasies. She never could have imagined how much she would love him or how wonderful it was to be loved so completely.

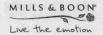

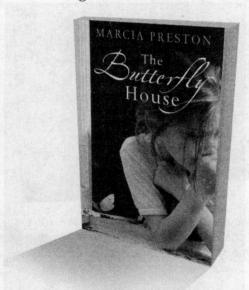